Also by James Castagno

———

Octavia and the Greek Key

Lady of the Lantern

Dance of the Red Panel

Out of Tunis
(early 2016)

WITNESS TO TERROR

James Castagno
A Novella

This is a work of fiction. All characters, businesses, places, events or incidents either are the products of the author's imagination or used in a fictitious manner. Any resemblance to actual persons, living or dead, or actual events is purely coincidental.

There is no witness so terrible and no accuser so powerful as conscience which dwells within us.

–Sophocles

I

THE HUNTERS

Carabinieri Captain Angelo Randi and U.S. Marshals Service Inspector Joe Costa, in official-looking dark suits, walked into the opulent bar at the Hotel Majestic, not far from Villa Borghese in central Rome.

The government sponsored conference on terrorism had ended thirty minutes earlier and Angelo knew Joe felt as he did. The presentation impressed neither of them.

Angelo motioned to the ornate vaulted ceiling and the large black leather bar stools. "Impressive isn't it?"

Joe raised his eyebrows and nodded.

They slipped onto chairs at the end of the bar and loosened their ties. The bartender, wearing his uniform of a short white tux jacket and bow tie, stepped up to take their order.

"Rémy Martin XO for both of us," Angelo said.

The conference was a waste of time, Angelo thought. An overabundance of politics, interwoven with European Union political correctness, turned him off after the first half hour. *A full day, time better spent tracking fugitives... wasted.*

"All bullshit. From the opening remarks, to the end," Angelo said.

Joe shrugged. "Affairs of state, nothing classified and no practical ideas on how to fight terrorism. We should have known."

The bartender set two perfectly filled crystal snifters in front of them and walked away.

Angelo rubbed his goatee. "Each month thousands of people from North Africa are given a free trip here, courtesy of the Italian Coast Guard. They don't carry Al Qaeda or ISIS identification cards. Thank God most of them go to northern Europe."

"Look at what my country is going through on the Mexican border. If the Middle East abutted our southern states, we'd be up to our asses in them. Who knows, we may already be." He lifted his glass. "Here's to yesterday's raid. The conference sucked, but at least we took five hardcore killers and a bomb maker off the streets," He tapped his glass against Angelo's and both sipped the expensive spirit.

Angelo set his drink on the bar and shook his head. "You had September eleventh... we've been lucky."

Joe took a deep breath and raised his eyebrows. "Hate to say it, but the day will come. The EU politicians won't turn anyone away. That decision will come back and bite them in the ass."

"Depressing, isn't it?" Angelo said as he tapped a fingernail against the crystal. "The sad part is they don't call us until after it's over, and the guy's hiding to keep his ass out of jail." He stared at Joe and rubbed his fingers across his goatee. "You never told me why you left Witness Security to chase wanted men around the world."

"Ten years dealing with psychopaths. Most of them would do anything to save their skin and remain free. Loved every minute spent working witnesses, but outwitting someone who doesn't want to be caught is more fun."

"Didn't you work at your headquarters?"

"Yeah, but the International Desk wasn't exciting enough, I wanted to get back on the street. Last year, when the Department of Justice announced the opportunity to come here and help you start the Fugitive Task Force, it didn't take me long to send in my application."

"Having family in Italy must have helped."

"No, but speaking Italian did." He took a short drink. "Let's talk about something more interesting. When are you going to introduce me to your wife's cousin?"

"Which one?" Angelo asked.

"The flight attendant you told me about last week. Why did you say she should have been a model?"

"Oh yes." Angelo raised his eyebrows. "Nina."

"Why modeling?"

Angelo smiled. He knew Joe wasn't a womanizer and had a strong connection to his family in Boston and the small town south of the Amalfi coast. "All the women in her family are taller than my wife."

"I wouldn't call Sofia short."

"No, but she looks up at Nina. How tall are you?"

"Six feet, two."

"Nina's three inches shorter."

"Wow." Joe's eyes brightened.

Angelo tilted his head and smiled. "Do you think my secretary has pretty eyes?"

"Mia? Hell yes, they're beautiful... she's beautiful."

"Nina's eyes are the same color, but a shade lighter."

Joe turned towards him and sat erect. "Why the hell are you waiting? Invite both of us to dinner so I can meet her."

"She's in London, but I know she wants to transfer back to Rome. I'll ask my wife."

II

THE PALESTINIAN

With all the pieces now in place, Saleh al-Filistini knew the western world would cower at the strength and boldness of those fighting the infidels. American soldiers throughout Europe would soon realize they met their match.

The sparse furnishing in the Milan apartment fit his goal to keep himself and his Saudi wife as inconspicuous as possible. The metropolitan area's large population of Middle Easterners aided him in maintaining a low profile. His slight English accent attracted little attention in the multicultural city.

He dropped onto the old couch, turned on the lamp and set a large manila envelope on the unfinished wooden coffee table. Saleh focused on Pasha, a man in his fifties in traditional Arab garb, sitting in a chair across from him.

Pasha's hands, folded on his lap, drew Saleh's eyes. The left hand, comprised of two fingers and a thumb, and the right, four scarred fingers and a thumb bent from multiple broken bones, made him shiver. *The hazard of being a bomb maker.* Saleh adjusted his shirt and leaned back. "How long have we been planning this?"

Pasha wiped sweat from his forehead. "More than one year."

When the sheik first proposed the mission to the terrorist leaders in Iran, Saleh had his doubts the operation was possible. His Al Qaeda boss in Tehran silenced him and supported the sheik in the same way a puppy would submit to its mother's demands. For the next six months, Saleh dampened the man's enthusiasm, bringing up the logistical problems and possible political ramifications of a bold bombing on mainland Europe. In spite of his misgivings, the day was at hand. He pressed his lips together and nodded to himself. *Finally, those left in the mountains along the Afghanistan border will get what they want.*

"The car is ready?" he asked Pasha.

"Yes. I finished it last night."

"Did you use the plastic explosive?"

Pasha continued to nod as he spoke. "Yes, Semtex... one kilo in a suitcase. It's easy to form and safe." He gazed around the room.

"Is something wrong?"

Pasha lowered his head and studied the square blue and white floor tiles. "I'm worried. We must be careful. This is Italy, not the streets of Kabul or Baghdad."

"You've done your job well, Pasha. You'll be gone before it happens. Remember to tell Nassem I will call him when I see the color of the bus."

Pasha's eyes remained on the tiles and he did not respond.

The Iraqi bomb maker was not someone Saleh wanted to befriend. The man scared him so much he no longer went to the small apartment where Pasha assembled the components of the bomb. He spoke of his destructive devices with the same loving words he used to describe his own children.

"You'll be rewarded, they transferred the money yesterday." Saleh lifted the envelope from the coffee table. "Put this in the car. Don't let Nassem see it."

"Why do you want to keep it hidden from the boy?"

"There's no reason for him to know who is on the bus." He pushed himself up from the couch.

Pasha stood, adjusted his calf-length thawb and took the envelope. "Peace be with you." He scurried out the door.

Saleh focused on the floor as he paced the living room. He pulled a cell phone from the pocket of his pressed slacks, dialed a number and waited.

Tomorrow's bold undertaking, hatched in the caves of Afghanistan, taxed his knowledge of operational planning. He had rehashed the details in his mind many times. *Flawless.* He knew Akram would pass the information to the sheik, waiting for word in the northern tribal area of Pakistan.

The ring on the phone stopped, and he listened to the voice asking the caller to leave a message. "We're ready, Akram. Tomorrow the world will hear and fear us."

The next morning, Saleh parked his black BMW at the side of a narrow two-lane mountain road overlooking a small Italian town, and reached for the binoculars on the passenger's seat.

He climbed from the car, set the field glasses on the roof and leaned against the door. A sense of calm and ease came over him as he relaxed his muscles, drew in a breath of fresh mountain air, unbuttoned his sports coat and loosened his tie.

During the past three months, he'd spent considerable time searching for the perfect location along the route. Every Tuesday the bus took the same mountain road out of the Southern Limestone Alps known as the Dolomites. Four times in the past, he parked in the same spot and watched the bus enter one side of the community and leave from the other. The village had a single road leading through it. *One way in, one way out.*

Saleh raised the binoculars and focused on the winding two-lane road leading into the left side of the town. He scanned right, over the red tiled roofs, and picked up the road as it emerged from behind a large church steeple topped with a golden cross. Two hundred yards from that side of the village, he focused on a two-door faded blue Fiat, parked along the side of the road.

At no time in his life had killing himself entered Saleh's mind. *How can the boy want to end his life?* Too many young, uneducated, fanatics spent their days studying in a radical madrasah. *Without them, Al Qaeda could not flourish and we would have no martyrs.*

Saleh focused the binoculars on the car window.

Nassem's seventeenth birthday was weeks away, and he did not regret the decision he had made. Soon his family would be honored on the streets and in the marketplaces of Kabul.

He wiped his forehead and pulled his sweat-soaked shirt away from his skin. Reaching over the steering wheel, he repositioned the cell phone on the dashboard. His eyes darted across the interior of the car and settled on the passenger's seat. A wire ran from a small plastic cylinder, with a red button, to a suitcase on the back seat. He raised the deadly device and stared at it. When his hand shook, he returned the cylinder to the seat beside him.

Staff Sergeant Tony Drago, a member of the 173rd Airborne Brigade Combat Team out of Vinceza Italy, sat behind the driver of the faded yellow tour bus with thin white stripes snaking their way across the front and along the sides. It eased around sharp curves on the two-lane road heading into the small town.

Thirty-four American soldiers, in uniform, occupied the seats behind Tony. The last week of mountain training with members of the Italian Army's 4th Alpini Parachutist Regiment had left them exhausted, and eager to get back to their base and routine duties. Most men dozed, but a few talked, or read newspapers and books while he gazed out the window. *Another two hours of boredom in a bus that looks like a ripe banana.*

He glanced at the driver and wondered how difficult it was to keep the bus on the proper side of the narrow winding pavement. The man, whose legs seemed too short to reach the pedals, tapped the brakes as they approached the edge of town.

III

THE FATAL DAY

Saleh's heart thudded in his chest as he lowered the binoculars and watched the yellow tour bus descend a hill from the left and disappear behind buildings at the edge of town. *Soon it will end. The news of Al Qaeda's terror will flow from Italy to Scandinavia.*

He removed the cell phone from his pocket, dialed a number and raised it to his ear. In the back of his mind, he debated if he should talk to the boy. "It's a large yellow bus. Be ready. It will soon pass you," he said into the phone and ended the call, not giving Nassem an opportunity to speak.

Saleh set the binoculars on the hood of his car and leaned against the fender. Crossing his arms over his chest, he kept his eyes on the right side of the town where his target would exit. His gaze moved to the Fiat, parked a short distance down the road.

###

Nassem adjusted himself in the seat and focused on the rear-view mirror. *The man on the phone must be somewhere nearby.* Movement on the road in front of his car caught his attention. A bus with large yellow stripes across the front sped towards him. He furrowed his brow and glanced back at the mirror. *Thought it would come from behind me.* As he lifted the cylindrical detonator from the passenger's seat, he shrugged and locked his eyes on the approaching target. *He said yellow... that's it.*

Saleh shook his head when he realized he had been staring at the road exiting town for over two minutes. Pushing himself away from the fender, he glanced at Nassem's car and spotted a tourist coach approaching the Fiat from the wrong direction.

A sinking feeling grew inside him as he grabbed the field glasses and raised them to his eyes. It took a few seconds to focus on the bus and the large yellow stripes on the front and sides. *It's almost the same color.* His mouth fell open, face contorted, and he dropped the binoculars. He struggled to remove his cell phone from his pocket and press the green button twice. With wide eyes locked on the bus speeding toward the Fiat, he held his breath, and listened to the phone ring. "Answer it!"

Nassem jumped in his seat the moment the phone rang. He reached to grab it, looked at the bus and lowered his hand. *I know... I see it.*

The coach did not slow down or move closer to the right edge of the road.

Nassem raised the detonator to his chest and glanced at the ringing cell phone. When he looked back at the bus, he saw the driver staring directly at him. As soon as it came alongside his car, he screamed, "Allahu Akbar" and pressed the red button.

Saleh flinched when he saw the bright flash of the explosion. "No!" He raced around the car, jumped in, and sped toward the small town.

He stopped at the side of the road, thirty meters behind a yellow tour bus. Saleh got out, stood beside the door and glared at a group of American soldiers, milling around a flat tire at the front of the bus. After he lowered himself back in the car, he stared at the men in uniform. "Today you were lucky. I was not."

Saleh slammed his fist onto the steering wheel, his lips pressed into a fine line. *Two motor coaches... almost the same color... coming from opposite directions. How could this happen?* "I hope it was empty and not full of Italian pensioners." He knew there would be no second opportunity to kill the Americans. He made a U-turn, and five minutes later, pulled onto the road to Milan.

IV

TRAGEDY

Staff Sergeant Drago and two soldiers turned away from the bus driver, cussing in Italian at the flat tire. "Look at that," Drago said pointing to a cloud of smoke rising above the buildings at the far side of town.

A Municipal Police officer got out of his compact Alfa Romeo, stepped to the center of the street and looked at the smoke.

The corporal standing beside Drago turned to him. "What the hell happened?"

A wide-eyed private held his hand out and shook it. "Damn ground vibrated."

Drago glanced from side to side and frowned. "Sounded like something exploded." He scanned the crowd of soldiers and located Lieutenant Rickter. "You hear that, sir?"

"Yeah," Rickter said and pointed at the police officer. "Find out what happened."

Drago trotted to the officer. "Excuse me."

"Yes."

"Do you know what happened?"

The officer looked at the smoke. "I'm going to find out."

"You're alone, can I go with you?"

"Yes." He headed to his car.

Drago turned and yelled. "Lieutenant, I'm going with him."

The patrol car stopped five feet from a gaping hole in the pavement. Both men momentarily froze in their seats. "Something exploded," Drago said.

Twisted car parts lay in the street and white sheets of paper littered the ground. A motor coach leaned against the far side of the ditch. Black smoke rose from a massive hole in its side.

The police officer and Drago leapt from the car and ran toward the wreckage.

Drago stopped at the edge of the road and his mouth fell open. He held an arm out to stop the police officer.

"Mother of God, what happened?" the officer asked. He pointed at two small bodies lying in the grass. "Children."

Drago scanned the massive hole in what used to be the side of the bus and clutched his stomach at the sight of young broken bodies inside the wreckage. "They're all children."

The officer raised a trembling hand to his forehead. "How did it happen?"

Images of the damage he had seen caused by improvised explosive devises in Afghanistan shot through Drago's mind. He dropped to one knee and glanced at car parts and an engine in the road. He turned and locked his eyes on jagged metal bent inward along the edge of the hole in the coach. "A car exploded beside the bus." A charred paper beside him fluttered in the breeze. He picked it up and saw half the page covered in Arabic writing. Drago folded the paper and shoved it in his pocket.

The officer squatted next to him and covered his mouth with his hand. "How could a car explode with such force?"

Drago rose. "It couldn't. This was a car bomb." As he and the officer walked past the wreckage, he picked up another page. "Here, it's written in Arabic. I think you need to call your headquarters." They reached the back of the bus and looked at the words written below the rear window. Drago's mouth fell open and his eyes widened when he read the bold black print. "Holy shit!"

V

REALIZATION

Saleh stepped into his apartment and marched to his computer on the coffee table. He dropped onto the couch, opened the laptop and hit the power button.

Twelve months of planning and surveillance wasted. There had never been another bus on the road during the times he watched the American soldiers returning to their base in Vicenza. *Why didn't Nassem answer the phone? That bus came from the wrong direction, he should have known.*

He typed an Internet address into the browser. The screen flashed to the World Caliphate website, and he focused on the words in the middle of the screen, reading them aloud. "A martyr has given of himself and destroyed infidels in Italy. Slay them wherever you find them, for persecution is worse than life without honor." Muscles stiffened, and he slammed his fist against the table. "Couldn't they wait to tell the world? The soldiers are still alive. A meaningless operation." Saleh took a deep breath and shook his head. Many times in the past he had seen the fools who maintained the website jump to conclusions that later turned out to be untrue. He closed the computer, leaned back and thought about the time and energy he and Pasha had wasted. *Something will be on the news.* He picked up the television remote and sat up to watch the state-owned RAI News 24 channel.

A video panning along the side of the smoldering wreck came on the screen. The raw footage showed firefighters spraying water on the bus. The video moved past the hole in the side of the bus and reached the back. An unfocused view of writing below the large back window appeared. The camera zoomed in and the fuzzy words became clear. Saleh thrust himself forward and read the words. "Centro Islamico, Milano, Italia." His eyes widened as his face turned to a mask of terror. "May the Prophet be merciful... what have I done?"

A female voice broke the silence of the broadcast. "Authorities estimate there may have been over thirty Muslim boys, nine to thirteen years old, and an unknown number of adults on the bus from the Milan Islamic Center. RAI News is waiting for a statement from the leading Iman in Milan."

Saleh's hands flew to his chest, and he gasped. Sudden coldness entered his core and his heart raced as the word 'children' repeatedly slammed into his head. A wail, that didn't sound human, poured out of his throat.

Most Fridays he visited the Islamic Center to pray. He knew the Iman and many Muslim faithful who frequented the end of the week service. For the past two years, he had purchased the uniforms for the youth soccer team. *I may have killed friends, destroying the dreams of families.*

The front door creaked opened, and he heard his wife and brother-in-law speaking.

"Thank you, Musa," Zarina said.

"I'm your brother... no need to thank me. I'll see you tomorrow."

The door closed and Zarina, wearing slacks, a long sleeve blouse and light jacket, stepped into the living room. She removed the hijab covering her head, let her black hair fall over her shoulders and glanced at the television. "What are you watching?"

Saleh did not respond nor turn his eyes from the TV.

She sat beside him and raised her eyebrows the second she saw his face. "What's wrong?" She glanced back at the television.

A tear slid down his cheek and he took her hand. "We need to pray for the children."

"What children?"

"Why must we try to kill everyone who does not follow Islam? We are destroying ourselves Zarina... we are destroying a great religion."

Zarina blinked and squinted. "Why are you talking this way?"

Saleh thrust a finger at the newscast. "Pasha's bomb killed Muslim children. The bus is in pieces." He lowered his head and focused on the floor. "It's time to stop the madness."

Zarina squinted and tilted her head. "Pasha returned to Baghdad... what Muslim children?"

"I did it Zarina!" He said as he leapt from the couch. "The mission I planned for over a year failed. The Afghan boy set off the bomb next to a bus carrying children from our Islamic Center." He walked away from her. "Leave me, I must call Tehran."

Zarina covered her mouth and ran to the kitchen.

Saleh pulled his cell phone from his pocket, scanned his contacts, tapped the screen and turned on the speaker.

After the third ring, Akram answered. "Peace be with you, Saleh."

"And with you, Akram. We are cursed."

There was a pause before Akram spoke. "I saw the news on the television. Everyone will understand this was not what you intended. Sometimes mistakes are made in the name of Islam."

Saleh's empty hand made a fist as blood rushed to his head and his face reddened. "Mistake? Over thirty Muslim boys died. We killed them... remember that, Akram."

"Maybe you should have been more observant."

Saleh glared at the phone. *I was and I see what is happening.* "The Prophet sent a message, a sign of what our future will bring."

"Often the innocent must die."

Saleh's fist tightened. "No, Akram. These were our children. Listen to yourself."

Akram sighed. "Listen to what I..."

"You said innocent! That means the boys were pure and uncorrupted by evil."

"Why are you shouting at me?"

Saleh forcibly exhaled and drew a short breath, his voice softened. "You are not listening. Those young lives mean nothing to you. I now know who is evil and corrupt."

"It is your duty to do what we ask and support our cause."

"I thought it was, but we kill our own people, defile our religion and destroy its future."

"That is not what we do, Saleh. Our purpose and goal is to bring Islam to the world."

"By force?" Saleh yelled. "No. I'm not here to destroy our youth. It's not the life I want for myself. I will no longer do this, I'm finished."

"You are our leader in Southern Europe."

"Find someone else, I can't live with the pain we inflict on innocent families."

Akram hesitated. "My friends and I will not allow you to leave us."

Saleh heard the subtle threat in the Al Qaeda's leader's voice. He opened his fist and stared at four curved marks of blood his fingernails had brought to the surface of his palm.

"You can't stop me, Akram. No one can. The Prophet produced peace from the cruelty of war. It's time I help him."

VI

THE PAPERS

Carabinieri Captain Angelo Randi brushed a piece of lint from his dark blue uniform and sat in a padded chair in front of Colonel Giuseppe Aldo's ornate oversized desk. He ran his hand through his black hair and glanced at the four rows of medals and a parachutist badge on Aldo's uniform. On the wall behind the desk, hung a framed photo of the colonel's father, a Carabinieri officer that helped arrest Benito Mussolini, in July 1943.

The colonel has good taste. Although Angelo had been in the office many times, the size and elegance of the furnishings impressed him. The round hand-forged iron coffee and end tables, next to the large couch, held slabs of rare black marble, no longer found in the Tuscan town of Carrara.

Aldo rubbed a hand over his shaved head, leafed through photos of the destroyed bus, raised one and shook it.

"Tonight there will be riots in the major cities of the Middle East."

Angelo shifted his stocky frame in the chair and nodded. "It was not intentional, they hit the wrong bus. They'll do everything in their power to turn their mistake into an advantage." He handed Aldo a piece of paper with a burned corner. "This is Al Qaeda's statement I told you about," he said handing his boss a second page. "Here's the translation."

Aldo read the sheet in Italian and shook his head. "The children didn't have a chance. Their bus came down that road at the wrong time."

"And the American soldiers were lucky their bus had a flat tire," Angelo added.

Aldo handed the paper in Arabic back to him and shoved the photos across the desk. "We need answers. You and Inspector Costa get everyone in the fugitive squad on this case. It's out of the ordinary since we don't know the identity of the people who did it, but your men are good at digging up information. Call your American contacts at the embassy and find out what the CIA knows. Tell Costa to set up a meeting. Al Qaeda tried to hit the bus full of American soldiers, their

Justice Department will want to get their hands on whoever did it."

Angelo slid his chair back.

"Take whatever resources you need and find the bastards." Aldo raised the translated page. "I'll have this copied and released to the press. The world needs to know they killed their own children."

That afternoon at the U. S. Embassy, Angelo sat across the conference table from FBI Agent Robert Duffy, in a room with no windows and bare walls. His partner, Inspector Joe Costa, had called earlier and said he'd be with the American ambassador in Milan, and wouldn't be able to come to the meeting. Duffy wasn't Angelo's first or second choice to meet. He was the only agent available.

Angelo opened his briefcase and removed copies of pages printed in Arabic and Italian.

"Since American soldiers were the target, we'd like to work with you on this," Duffy said.

Angelo cocked his head to the side. "Who do you mean?"

"The Bureau... the FBI."

"You?" *The one they jokingly call 'The Kid' behind his back?*

"Yeah."

The young FBI agent grated on Angelo's nerves. All the other American agents had many years of service with their respective agencies and were veterans of complicated international investigations. Robert graduated law school and joined the FBI four years ago. The young man could not stop talking about the wonders of the FBI and the heroics of his uncle, the Executive Assistant Director for Science and Technology.

Angelo pressed his lips together and nodded. "Joe Costa helped us set up our task force, and he's already involved... but of course. I'll ask Colonel Aldo to get you clearance."

The door opened and a wiry gray-haired man, carrying a pair of glasses and a thick folder, entered the room. Angelo, well aware of the man's reputation, never met him, but had heard the stories of the beautiful female Russian agent he convinced to defect.

The man nodded. "Hi, Robert."

Angelo and Duffy stood.

The man extended his hand. "Captain Randi, I'm Al Provitti."

"Please, call me Angelo."

"Sit and we'll get started." Al said. He slid a folder, stamped in red with CIA Top Secret, onto the table. He peered over the glasses perched on the tip of his nose.

"Angelo leads the Carabinieri Fugitive Task Force," Duffy said.

"Yes. I've worked with his boss."

"I hope you can help us," Angelo said placing his hand on the two pages in front of him. "These are the papers found near the bus. We need all the information we can get."

"I have copies of those," Al said pointing to the papers. He tapped the folder in front of him. "This should give you a good start... sources redacted. Do you know Josef Alfano... a section chief at your government's External Information and Security Agency?"

"A.I.S.E.? Yes, I spoke to him once."

"He and I share information. He has copies of everything I'm giving you. I believe it's best if you get your information from him. Please understand, I don't want to step on anyone's toes in the Italian intelligence community."

"Yes, and I respect that. I'll call him."

"Is Inspector Costa and your task force involved?" Al asked.

"Yes. Colonel Aldo told us to make this case our top priority."

Al removed the contents from the folder and pushed the papers across the table.

Angelo looked at the documents. "Our people think they used the explosive Semtex. Any way to find out where it came from?"

Al raised his eyebrows and shook his head. "It wouldn't matter. Czechoslovakia sent so much of it to the Middle East it's as common as shit under a fly's feet."

Angelo hid his smile. "Have you intercepted any communications?"

"Not yet. They're staying quiet. I'm sure you saw their website before they changed it. They're now blaming the Italian government."

"The Prime Minister will not stay quiet."

"I don't blame him," Duffy said. "He needs to schedule a news conference as soon as possible."

Angelo noticed Al roll his eyes.

"Good idea," Al said.

Duffy doesn't get it... he never does, Angelo thought.

Provitti handed him a business card.

He glanced at it and raised his eyes to him. "Military Attaché?"

The CIA Station Chief repositioned his glasses on his nose and shrugged. "Everyone needs to be called something. Military Attaché sounds better than cook and bottle washer, and it has immunity attached to it. I'll speak with Alfano and tell him to expect your call."

VII

CARMINE AND THE TEENAGER

Along the dark street, two of Akram's men sat in a black car, parked under a tree twenty yards from the entrance to Saleh's apartment. The man in the passenger seat held a folding stock AK-47 rifle and listened to the drone of the motor.

They scrunched down when a white Smart Fortwo rolled past and parked in front of the apartment. A young woman, and a Middle Eastern man, got out and walked to the front door. She shoved the key into the lock.

"Now, before they go inside." the passenger said.

The driver slipped from the parking spot with the lights off, stopped in front of the apartment and the shooter raised the weapon. Ten shots, in rapid succession, shattered the silence along the street.

###

Zarina spun around at the sound as bullets slammed into Musa, the doorframe, and the side of the house. He grabbed her blouse as he fell, ripping it and exposing her shoulders and red bra.

Zarina's face contorted. She yanked the hijab from her head and screamed, sinking to her knees beside him.

Tires squeals and a car sped down the street.

She wiped her cheek, not realizing she was spreading his blood across her face. "Musa, get up." Her pulse raced and heart pounded when she saw him gasp and his head fall to the side. "Musa! No!" She lowered her head to his chest.

Saleh, standing in his living room, recognized the unmistakable sound of gunfire and ran to the front of the apartment. He yanked open the door and froze when he saw his wife on her knees leaning against her brother's red stained shirt. He pulled her away from Musa. "Have you been shot?"

"No, my brother!"

He glanced at tears mixing with blood on her cheeks and his eyes widened as he focused on her exposed hair, bare shoulders and bra. "Get in the house and close the door," he said pulling her to her feet.

Zarina pushed him. "No, Musa..."

"Cover yourself," Saleh yelled. He shoved her into the apartment and slammed the door.

His Italian neighbor, Carmine, with his teenage son, ran to Saleh's side. "We called the police," the teenager said. He glanced at Musa. "Holy Jesus, look at the blood."

Carmine squatted and pressed two fingers against Musa's bloody neck. "I'm sorry. I think he's dead."

Saleh looked down the street when he heard the fluctuating wail of a siren. A police car, with two flashing blue strobe lights on the roof, sped toward the house. Behind him, the door opened and Zarina stood in the doorway sobbing. With one hand, she held a scarf covering her hair. The other hand clamped the torn fabric of her blouse against her neck. Tears flowed over smeared makeup and blood.

Saleh stared at her and tightened his jaw. "Go inside the house!" He forced her into the apartment and pulled the door closed.

Two officers from the Italian National Police ran up the walkway. The tall one arrived first and the short man followed, barking orders. "Move out of the way... everyone get back."

The tall officer stepped beside Musa and looked at his body. He turned and glared at Saleh. "Who lives here?"

Saleh placed his hand over his heart. "I do."

The officer turned to Carmine. "Who are you?"

"We live next door. I work in a medical clinic." He pointed at Musa. "I checked. He's dead... no pulse."

The officer looked at Saleh. "Your name?"

"Saleh... Saleh al-Filistini."

"Do you know this man?" He pointed to the body.

"He's my brother-in-law."

Both police officers looked to the street as a black Alfa Romeo, with a blue flashing light on the dash, pulled to a stop.

Carabinieri Lieutenant Massimo Scopise, in his distinctive dark blue uniform, approached the apartment. His driver raced around the car and followed five feet behind his boss.

Carmine and his son stepped away from the body.

Massimo looked at the tall police officer and nodded. "Good evening, Franco, we received a call. Did anyone see this happen?"

Franco snapped to attention. "Yes, sir, the dead man's brother-in-law, Saleh."

Saleh shook his head. "No, my wife did, she's in the apartment." He leaned to Musa and touched his head. "Peace my brother."

"What is your full name?" Massimo asked.

"Al-Filistini, Saleh."

"Please tell your wife to come out." He turned to his driver. "Call this in to headquarters."

Massimo stared at Saleh and waited for a reply. After ten seconds he said, "Get your wife."

Saleh shuffled his feet. "She's Muslim, she must stay in our home."

I'm in no hurry, Massimo thought looking into Saleh's eyes. He spoke in a low confident tone. "You speak with a British accent?"

Saleh's eyes darted to Musa and back to Massimo. "I went to school in London."

"Then understand, you are in Italy, and you are subject to the laws of the Republic. Where are you from?"

"Palestine."

Massimo leaned toward him. "In Gaza would I have to abide by their laws?"

"Yes."

"Then I suggest you get your wife."

Saleh pushed open the door.

A woman stood in the hall with glassy eyes and smeared makeup. Her long sleeve blouse, buttoned to the neck. Wrapped over her head and around her neck, a scarf, covered her hair. She held a red cell phone at her side.

Saleh took a deep breath. "Please, can we go inside the house?"

Massimo followed Saleh and the woman to the couch. He remained standing, pulled out a pad and pen and scribbled notes. He looked at her. "Your name, madam?"

"Zarina."

Massimo tilted his head forward, focused on her and raised his eyebrows.

"Al-Ansari... Zarina al-Ansari," she said.

"And the man shot is your brother?"

"Yes," Saleh said.

Massimo turned to him. *He's in control.* His eyes lingered on Saleh, then turned back to Zarina. "What is your brother's name?"

"Musa Gafar al-Ansari," she said.

Massimo took his time. "Did you see who killed him?"

"No."

"Your husband said you did."

"I was standing with him, when someone shot from a car." She sobbed and placed a hand over her mouth. "He fell in front of me."

"Why would anyone want to kill him?"

Saleh slid close to his wife. "She wouldn't know that."

Massimo rubbed his goatee and stared at Saleh. "Mr. al-Filistini, I am speaking to your wife."

Saleh raised a hand. "People in Iran want me killed."

"Then why did they kill him?"

"I don't know."

Sure he does, he doesn't want to tell me. He noticed Zarina's eyes open wide, and she adjusted her position on the couch, her lips pursed.

Saleh glanced at her and turned to Massimo. "My wife knows nothing about it."

She stared at him and tightened her jaw.

Massimo thought the couple odd. In past dealings with Muslims, they cooperated for fear it would affect their immigration status and they may face deportation. *He must have a resident permit, he doesn't seem concerned.* "Why should I believe you are telling me the truth?"

Saleh's eyes narrowed, and he clenched his teeth. "Call the CIA, MI-6 or your A.I.S.E. Ask them if they have heard the name Mohammad Halabi."

Zarina's eyes widened and a seething look of disgust came over her face as she turned away.

The moment the words came out of Saleh's mouth, Massimo concluded he would not be leaving the house soon. *This guy must be someone's spy.* He motioned to a nearby chair. "May I sit?"

Saleh nodded.

Massimo dragged the chair to the coffee table and noticed Zarina's demeanor had turned from sorrow to anger. He made notes on the pad.

VIII

MOHAMMAD HALABI

Angelo leaned his high backed leather chair away from the desk, folded his arms over his chest, and stared across the office. Two padded chairs and a small couch surrounded a low table in front of his desk. *We always know who we're looking for, where the hell do we start?*

The telephone rang. "Hello." He listened a moment. "Yes, Mia, bring it here."

When his secretary entered the office, he smiled. *Single and a beautifully built man magnet.* He knew she realized most men and women sensed her presence when she walked into a room, but Angelo was different. She was one of his wife Sofia's many cousins.

She handed him a two-page report and sauntered out.

As he read the report, his eyes stopped on the name Halabi. He dropped the pages, lifted the phone handset and tapped two numbers. "Mia, this report is dated yesterday.

When did it arrive in our office?" His gaze slid from side to side as he listened. "Okay. Find Lieutenant Scopise... he's in Milan. Get him on the phone."

Al Provitti sat at his desk in a windowless office and picked up a folder stamped 'Top Secret' just as the phone rang. He hit the speakerphone button. "Yes, Julia."

Al trusted his secretary with his life. She had never failed him. Although she could have retired a year ago, he considered himself lucky she loved her job and wanted to remain in Rome.

"General Alfano is on the line," she said.

"General?" He heard Julia chuckle. "Put him through."

"Go ahead, sir," Julia said.

"So, you're a general now?" Al said as he leaned back and clamped his hands behind his head.

"I thought by now you would have received the news. Did the CIA lose contact with the outside world?" Alfano asked.

"Josef, you're not political enough to be a general."

"That's true. It would be nice but I'm happy with my present position."

"What can I do for you?"

"Nothing, but I received a report from Milan and I can make this the best day of your life."

Al smiled. "Are you going to introduce me to Miss Italy tonight?"

"I'm no fool, I'd keep her for myself. But I know someone you are dying to meet."

"This has got to be good. Who might that be?"

"Al Qaeda's man in Southern Europe... Mohammad Halabi."

Al laughed and leaned forward. He directed his soft voice toward the speakerphone. "Damn Josef, this may be the best one you ever pulled."

To survive in the job, those in the intelligence services needed to have a good sense of humor. Al's Italian counterpart had the reputation of a man who could convince a Ferrari owner to trade his legendary sports car for a Volkswagen.

"You're blowing smoke up my ass. No one knows what he looks like."

"You're correct. Only the photo of his back while sitting with bin Laden outside a cave, but I am now looking at a copy of his Italian driver's license."

Al sat up in his chair. "You serious?"

"We should have him in custody by the end of the day."

A thousand questions bounced around Al's brain. *How the hell did they find him?* "Do we get to talk to him?"

"Consider this call your invitation."

"Call me when you get him and we'll meet."

"I will." Josef ended the call.

Al hit the speakerphone button and dialed. "Julia?"

"Yes."

"Get someone near the top at the Directorate of Intelligence on the phone."

"Which office?"

"Any of them... No! Terrorism Analysis."

"Sir, it's almost midnight in Washington."

"I know... it's important. I don't want to talk to the Duty Officer. Tell him to get a person well above his pay grade out of bed. Make sure he has a STE secure telephone and get his number. I'll call him... no wait. First get me the Mohammad Halabi file, then make the call."

IX

THE DISAPPEARANCE

Angelo made it from Rome to Milan with ten minutes to spare. He met Lieutenant Scopise just before a group of officers approached the apartment they knew to be rented by Saleh al-Filistini, also known as Mohammad Halabi.

Earlier in the day Angelo talked to Massimo on the phone. The lieutenant explained that he hadn't recognized the name and didn't know an arrest warrant had been issued for Saleh in the name Halabi. After Saleh mentioned the intelligence agencies, he assumed the guy worked for one of them.

Angelo and Scopise walked to the side of the building and leaned against the wall near the door. Both men watched an officer thrust a ram against the deadbolt and step aside. Five officers rushed into the apartment.

Two minutes later, an officer came to the door "They're gone. It looks like they were in a hurry."

"Talk to the neighbors, get as much information as you can," Massimo said.

Angelo frowned and shook his head. It wasn't their fault. Someone at Carabinieri headquarters had taken their time forwarding Massimo's report. The name Mohammad Halabi wasn't well known outside the intelligence community. He had recognized it because of the old wanted fugitive file. *Why would he identify himself and then leave? It makes little sense.*

Angelo pulled his cell phone from his pocket and dialed. "He's not here. Find out if he has a car."

"Are you going back to Rome?" Massimo asked.

"Yes."

"I'll make sure everyone in Milan knows he's wanted."

###

Akram, and Gafar Muhammad al-Ansari, Zarina's father, sat at a cheap makeshift desk in a tiny Tehran street level office. Stains marked the walls where old posters and papers had once hung. A stack of magazines and newspapers lay on a square wooden table across the room.

Akram looked at Gafar's traditional Saudi Arabian dress. A cord circlet held a diagonally folded cloth on his skullcap.

"When do you return to Riyadh?" Akram asked.

"As soon as possible. We're waiting for the Italians to release Musa's body. My family needs me."

"Did you hear anything more?"

Gafar looked at the floor and shook his head. "Nothing. My wife is worried about Zarina."

"How could Saleh be so stupid?" Akram asked.

"Stupid?"

"Two different buses... soldiers and children. All he had to do was look."

"I was speaking of Zarina, not Saleh. She must not be hurt. Those who killed my son cannot hide from me forever."

"Did you try to call her?"

"Yes, the phone is disconnected."

Akram knew losing one of his sons had dealt a blow to Gafar's family. *Praised be Allah, no one told him I sent the two men to Saleh's house.* "I am sorry about your son. Those who killed him were not competent. I've contacted my best men in Italy. They're discreet and efficient, and will soon find him."

"What about the bank account?"

"If he moves the money, I'll be notified and told where it went."

Gafar leaned over the desk and stared at Akram. "The sheik wants him found."

"Doesn't he understand we're trying?"

"Yes, but the longer it takes, the more trouble we both face. Why did I agree when she married an educated refugee?"

"Your daughter made a better life for herself. She is not hiding with the tribes in North Waziristan."

"Palestinian... why a Palestinian?" Gafar asked himself.

"She has always had her own mind."

Gafar stared at him. "My family will find those who murdered Musa. I do not want Zarina harmed. If she is hurt, people will die."

"You have my word, Gafar. Saleh is the target. Continue trying to call her."

X

ROME IS SAFE

Normally a six-hour trip, it took Saleh five hours to drive to Rome. He and Zarina sat on the couch in the living room of a hotel suite on via National near Piazza Repubblica in central Rome. Saleh stared at the wall across the room. Without turning his head, he sensed her glaring at him.

"I still don't understand why you gave the police that name... have you gone mad?" her voice tight with anger.

He looked at her and thought about how he had explained himself hours ago. Another argument was not what he wanted. "Everything is different now. It's time to stop killing."

"You can't quit. You're abandoning our cause."

"When I saw the newscast of the children, I knew the prophet had spoken."

Zarina raised her voice. "The prophet was a fierce warrior."

She's starting again, calm yourself. "Yes, I know, but he was also a teacher."

Zarina slid away from him. "You'll dishonor your family."

"What family, they're all dead."

"Because of you, my father will die."

"Gafar knows the right people, nothing will happen to him."

"What about my sister and my other brother?"

"Those men were after me not Musa. The rest of you are safe. You know he died because someone believed I was the one standing with you at the door."

Zarina tilted her head and stared at him.

"It was a sign, Zarina, just like the children."

A knock on the door startled them. Saleh jumped to his feet, reached for her hand and pulled her from the couch. "Go in the bedroom." He waited for her to close the bedroom door. After he looked through the peephole, he relaxed, and opened the door, blocking the entrance to the room with his body.

A hotel employee leaned on a serving cart. "Your food sir, may I bring it into your room?"

"No, I'll take it." Saleh pulled the cart into the room and closed the door.

Zarina stepped from the bedroom and followed him as he pushed it to a small circular table. He lifted a bottle of water from the tray on the cart. "I'll be back in an hour."

She grabbed his arm and glared at him. "Where are you going, you can't leave me here alone?"

He took her hand and patted it. "Don't leave the room or answer the door. I won't be long. We need to get the money out of the Swiss account before Akram takes it. The bank's not far."

On his way to the door, Saleh picked up a briefcase setting beside the wall.

Angelo and Duffy sat in chairs beside the low table in Angelo's office. He handed Duffy a sheet of paper. Colonel Aldo had told him the Fugitive Task Force and the Counterterrorist Group would find al-Filistini. Until the request from the FBI received approval, he was to spoon-feed them information. Based on Aldo's words, Angelo knew it may take a while for the paperwork to reach a Lieutenant General exercising overall control over the Regional Commanders. *Inspector*

Costa is working with us, what more can the American Justice Department ask?

"Where's Costa?" Duffy asked.

"He's working with a few of my men."

"So you think this guy al-Filistini's driving a black BMW."

"That's what the neighbors said."

Duffy scanned the page. "Why would he give the lieutenant the name Halabi if he planned to run?"

"I don't know. Assuming we're right that Al Qaeda sent men to kill him, he had to get out of that apartment. When he gave us that name, he may have been thinking about talking, but reconsidered. If Provitti's friend Josef Alfano is correct, and Saleh's friends in Iran want him dead, we need to find him first... alive."

"And convince him we're the only ones who can keep him that way. Why don't I get one of our SWAT teams over here?"

Angelo raised his eyebrows. *All we need is a bunch of cowboys with guns on our streets.* "Such a proposal would need approval at the highest level of the government. You and

I will retire before that happens. We'll find him." *Call your uncle, he'll fix everything.*

Mia stepped into the room carrying two demitasses of espresso and set them on the table in front of the two men. "Hello, Mr. Duffy."

"Please, Mia, call me Robert. You get more beautiful each time I see you."

He doesn't stand a chance, Angelo thought.

Mia smiled. "Thank you." She walked to the door and stopped. "Angelo, are you and Mr. Duffy going to be long?"

"No."

She nodded and stepped from the office.

Duffy sighed and raised his eyebrows.

"She's still not married," Angelo said.

"I'm not the marrying type."

Angelo shrugged. "Then you have no chance with her."

"Maybe dinner, we'll see."

Angelo laughed. *The guy is acting like Giacomo Casanova and his name doesn't even end in a vowel.* "Dinner, possibly, but you can forget dessert. So, back to our missing Palestinian. By tonight, every police officer in Italy will look for him."

###

Saleh returned the hotel room, set down his briefcase, and eyed the cart of untouched food. Zarina, on the couch, held the television remote and bounced between channels.

"You didn't eat?"

"The pasta isn't good. You said it wouldn't take long. Where were you? It's been two hours. Did you get the money?"

"No. It will take a day to gather that much cash and the bank in Zurich must approve the withdrawal. They said the day after tomorrow."

"Can we go for pizza?"

"Why don't you eat the food I ordered?"

"I don't like it."

Saleh felt a headache coming on, took a deep breath and shook his head. "I'll get pizza." He headed toward the door.

"Nothing from the hotel... a good one," Zarina said.

###

Saleh strolled out the double doors of the hotel and stopped to let a deliveryman, carrying three large bags of coffee, pass in front of him.

Every muscle in his body tensed at the sound of automatic rifle fire. The bags erupted, spewing dark beans across the sidewalk. The deliveryman spun and crumbled in front of him, blood seeping from the man's body. A split second later Saleh dove to the ground at the second crack of rifle fire.

Bullets ricocheted off the sidewalk, tore into the hotel door and shattered windows. Saleh's face contorted in terror as he low-crawled across pieces of glass, threw himself against the door and into the hotel lobby.

He jumped to his feet and raced past a stunned clerk and a screaming couple kneeling on the floor in front of the check-in desk. On his way up the three flights of stairs, he wiped his blood splattered hands on his shirt.

Saleh burst into the hotel suite. Crushed coffee beans clung to his pants around the rips in the fabric at his knees. "Zarina!"

She ran from the bedroom and stopped. Her eyes widened and hand covered her mouth. "What happened? You're bleeding!" She tightened her hands around his arm.

Saleh yanked his arm away, ran to the bedroom and picked up a towel from the bed. He wiped his hands and face, threw the towel on the floor and snatched open dresser drawers. With both hands he scooped up his clothes and threw them on the bed. "Pack your bag, we need to leave."

Zarina stared at him with her mouth open. "Are you bleeding? Your pants are ripped."

He grabbed his suitcase from the corner and shoved the clothes into it. "Someone tried to kill me, but it's not my blood."

"No one knows we're here!"

"Get your clothes! Akram knows."

An hour later they had avoided the police by going out the back service entrance of the hotel. They settled into a single room in a two-star hotel, near Piazza Navona and the Pantheon.

Zarina tapped her fingers on the wooden armrest of the one chair in the room and stared at Saleh sitting on the bed.

"Have you noticed anyone follow us from Milan?" he asked.

"I wasn't watching."

He understood why. She had been in a vile mood since they left Milan and dozed for most of the trip. She hadn't looked at him more than twice since they walked into the new hotel room. "You don't seem to be concerned that people are trying to kill us."

She stepped to him and took his hands. "Don't say that. I am concerned. We should call my father and ask for his help."

To him, the tragedy in the mountains meant more than a mistake. To her it was part of their quest to rid the world of infidels. *She thinks Akram and her father will again trust me. No reason to argue.* "Do you still want pizza?"

"Yes."

"What do you want on it?"

"You know what I like. While you are out, try to move the car closer to the hotel."

Saleh slipped on his shoes and headed to the door. "I'll be gone thirty minutes, stay in the room."

He walked out the hotel door and looked in both directions. No parking spaces were available near the entrance. Motorbikes took up more area than they needed. When he and Zarina arrived at the hotel, he had noticed a pizza restaurant at a nearby corner. He turned in that direction.

Saleh returned to the hotel room carrying a large pizza Margherita and set it on the low desk. "I bought your favorite."

Zarina, pulled the chair in front of the box. "Thank you."

"I don't understand how they could have known we came to Rome? Akram must have called all his men living in the city. We might recognize them if we pay more attention to the people around us," he said.

"What are we going to do?" she asked between bites.

He sighed and shook his head. "I don't know. We can't stay here long. I think somewhere in the country will be safer." He took a slice from the box.

"Did you move the car?"

"No." He stepped to the window overlooking the front of the hotel and pulled back the curtain. "All the parking spaces are taken. Maybe later."

"We need a plan, Saleh. There's no reason to move from hotel to hotel when we can find someplace safe. Why don't we leave Italy and go to Saudi Arabia?"

The piece of pizza in his hand stopped at his mouth. He stepped beside her and returned the wedge to the box. "Your father has been working for Al Qaeda since before your birth. He has too much to lose. I'm the last person he wants to help."

"What about me? Does what I want matter to you?"

Saleh sat on the edge of the desk. "Do you want to leave?"

"What do you mean?"

"Go back to Saudi Arabia... alone?"

Her body stiffened, and she reached out to touch his hand. "No, Saleh. My duty is to stay with you."

He kissed her on the cheek and grabbed the slice of pizza. *Finally she's being reasonable.*

They passed time watching television. Saleh looked out the window every thirty minutes checking for an empty slot to park his car. At half past ten, he saw a vacant space. He grabbed his keys. "There's an open spot to park, I'll move the car." He left the room and scurried down three flights of stairs. As he stepped out of the hotel, he paused and looked in both directions. A man sat in a chair, and talked on a phone, near a doorway fifty feet down the street. He watched him for a full minute, but the guy didn't look in his direction.

The tension in Saleh's body ebbed away, and he headed up the street past the motorbikes. When he reached the scooter at the end of the line, he heard a loud pop and saw smoke flow from the plastic travel box on the back of the bike. A fiery hole grew in the side of the box.

Saleh's muscles tensed, and his heart fluttered, as an icy chill ran down his spine He had seen it happen many times. A defective or damp blasting cap or detonator failed to set off the explosive and caused it to catch fire. The sound of a metal chair clanging against concrete made him turn. The man who had been on the cell phone, ran down the street and disappeared around a corner.

With short backward steps, he eased away from the bike keeping his eyes on the flames shooting from the hole in the travel box. He spun around and bolted to the hotel door.

XI

THE SUMMER HOUSE

Saleh and Zarina took less than an hour to leave the hotel and reach the SS-5 roadway, snaking its way toward the mountains near Tivoli, east of Rome.

Zarina focused on the dark road stretching out ahead of the BMW. "Where are we going?"

Saleh ignored her.

"How can we stay in Italy? We need to go to Riyadh."

Saleh turned and looked at her. "You are wasting your time, Zarina. Forget about Riyadh, forget about your father. Akram, and your father's friends, would like nothing more than to see me dead." He clamped his teeth together and took a deep breath through his nose.

"Even if his best friend asked, my father wouldn't hurt my husband."

The car rounded a curve and Saleh stiffened when he spotted the blue flashing lights of a police car at the side of the road. He glanced at Zarina.

They passed a traffic officer examining a parked motorcycle. As they went by, Saleh looked in the rear view mirror and held his breath when he saw the officer looking in their direction.

"Is he coming?" Zarina asked.

"No."

She focused out the windshield and pointed to a white and black street sign. "The town of Tivoli Terme is five kilometers." She turned and snapped at him. "This is the way to Musa's summer house."

"No one will think we went there."

In the rear view mirror, Saleh glimpsed flashing lights. "The police are behind us."

Zarina's eyes widened, and she glanced out the rear window.

When the officer's patrol car pulled behind them, Saleh slowed and waved for him to pass. High beam headlights flashed twice, illuminating the interior of the BMW.

The options Saleh had available raced through his mind. *I can't keep going. He'll use his radio.* He thought of no reason the officer should recognize him or the car. The Italian authorities would want to talk with him after he mentioned the name Halabi, but he didn't think they would pass the information to the local police. *What does he want?*

Saleh removed a Browning High Power semiautomatic pistol from the center console and transferred it to his left hand beside the door. He pulled to the side of road, stopped, and lowered his window.

The police officer approached the side of the car. "Good evening. The rear light on the left side of your car is not working."

"Sorry, I didn't notice."

The officer squinted and nodded. "Are you British?"

"Yes."

"This car has an Italian license plate."

"It belongs to a company owned by a friend."

"Is he Italian?"

"Yes."

The officer leaned to the window, looked at Zarina and nodded. "Good evening," he said, and looked back at Saleh. "May I see your identity documents?"

Saleh pointed at the glove-box. "Get our passports." He kept his left hand against the side of the door and turned to the officer. "Would you rather see my license?"

"No, those will suffice." He examined the two United Kingdom passports, scanning the entry and exit stamps of various countries. Leaning over he pointed at Zarina "And Zarina is your wife?"

"Yes."

"You both travel to the Middle East often."

"Business... imports to Italy, and to visit friends."

The officer handed him the passports. "Please repair the light tomorrow, Mr. Harrington."

"I will."

"Drive carefully, good night."

Saleh watched him walk to his car as he turned the BMW back onto the road and drove away.

Zarina exhaled. "I thought we would have to kill him."

Saleh's eyes lingered on her. *Too many years helping her father... no qualms about killing people.* "Why take the life of an innocent man?"

Zarina ignored his question.

Saleh stopped the car near the front door of a weathered stone house built on a deserted hillside. The headlights illuminated a dead plant in a clay pot beside the entrance. He left the lights on and they walked to the pot. Saleh shoved dirt aside, removed a plastic bag with a key in it and unlocked the door.

Zarina stepped inside the foyer, turned on the lights and set her handbag on the floor. She looked at drop cloths covering the furnishings.

"Uncover everything. I'll get the bags," Saleh said.

He returned with two suitcases, and the briefcase, and shook his head when he noticed Zarina, still standing in the foyer staring into the house. "Why are you doing nothing to help us?"

"I hate this place. Musa said he wanted to sell it."

He moved past her and entered the living room. "It's safe here, and you can cook what you want. I'll go to a market tomorrow."

Zarina slid beside him and took his hand. "Why are you doing this?"

"Have you listened to a single word I've said?" He raised his hands. "If you don't know by now, you'll never understand!"

"We worked so hard."

Saleh berated himself for not remaining calm. "I can no longer fight for Islam if it means killing more Muslims, especially children. How many lives and families are we to destroy in our lifetime?"

She stepped back and glared at him. "It's not only Muslims that die."

"How many must? A hundred times more than Jews or Christians?"

"We can't hide forever."

He reached out, held her shoulders and steadied his voice. "The Italians may help us."

Zarina shoved him. "Are you out of your mind? The Italians will kill us because of what happened to the children." She strode from the room.

XII

FIND HIM

Gafar and Akram sipped tea in the small office in Tehran.

"I don't think he's given the Italian authorities any information. Maybe he wants to go his own way," Gafar said.

"I told him we wouldn't allow it. My men tried to kill him at the hotel but Sky News reported that the Mafia killed someone. I think they were told what to say, it wasn't him."

Gafar took a deep breath. "Your men must be more cautious. There will be consequences if we keep killing people in Italy."

Akram tightened his jaw. "Do not question my resolve. I've spent many hours on the phone talking to our friends who know him. We'll find out where they moved."

Gafar didn't back down. He glanced at his fingers tapping against his knee and looked at Akram. "I didn't question your resolve. Your plans may open the eyes of the

Italian government. How many more of their citizens will die before he's killed?"

"You're naive. We will kill as many as it takes to save ourselves."

Gafar leaned over the table. "The decision is yours. Kill as many as you want but remember what I said about my daughter. Tell your men to be very careful before they shoot."

Al and Josef alternated paying the bill for their biweekly outings in downtown Rome. A year earlier Al proposed they meet away from the office to discuss anything they didn't want put on paper or being recorded. They also used the time to discuss the tribulations of life with teenage children.

Today's meeting, four days since the last, was out of the ordinary. Al had received printouts of intercepted communications, and that morning sent them to Josef's office.

They walked to a table at a sidewalk café not far from 'il Vittoriano', the monument to Victor Emmanuel II, hated by most Romans. Al knew Josef picked the spot because he loved the view of the magnificent white marble structure and its matching bronze statues of the goddess Victoria in chariots drawn by four horses, high atop the building.

"Coffee?" Josef asked.

"Yeah."

A young waitress stepped to the table and Al stared at the tattoo on her neck, two inches below her ear.

"Two coffees," Josef said.

The girl spun and hurried into the café.

Al shook his head. "Why would a girl have an ancient insignia of Rome tattooed there?"

Josef smiled. "S.P.Q.R., The Senate and the Roman people. She must study political science at the University of Rome."

Al rolled his eyes. "Kids. You read the Tehran telephone transcripts I sent you?"

Josef nodded and raised his eyebrows. "Yes, interesting. I've been tracking down the Italian numbers called."

"We both need to make sure the information doesn't get into the hands of law enforcement authorities too soon," Al said. "If they pick up people, the calls will stop."

Josef nodded. "I know you won't share it and neither will I. I didn't think they'd be this careless."

"If we wait long enough, and they continue to bullshit with each other, we'll have a list of their entire organization in Italy."

"When that time comes, people will scream." Josef raised his eyebrows. "A few of the numbers are attached to important names with good reputations."

Ms. SPQR slid two espressos on the table and dropped four packets of sugar. "Something to eat?"

Al handed her two Euros. "No thank you."

"Call if you want anything." She walked to the café door.

Once she was out of earshot, Josef leaned over the table. "Have you heard anything from..."

Al's phone rang. He raised a finger and answered it. "Hello... right now?" He glanced at Josef, pursed his lips, and continued his conversation. "Cause a commotion... keep him occupied." He began to turn toward the street but stopped. "Okay, when we leave, we'll take a look." He ended the call.

"What was that about?"

Al raised his hand. "Don't react. Someone followed us. We're being watched."

"How do you know?"

"Two of my agents have been keeping an eye on me."

"What do you want to do?"

Al grinned. "Finish our coffee, get in your car and drive away."

"They'll follow us."

"It's one man. He won't be able to follow. My people will take care of him."

"Where is he?"

"Across the street... in front of the news stand. When we walk to your car, we should be able to see him." Al rubbed his temple. "They'll keep him busy, but it would be great if you can have someone pick him up?"

"What do your men look like?"

"One is female... long blond hair and easy to pick out in a crowd."

"I'll call from inside." Josef marched into the café.

Al downed his coffee and tapped his fingers on the table while he waited for him to return. He knew the chances of the man being connected with the Halabi case were slim but not impossible. *Love to pick all that information from his brain.*

Josef approached the table and sat. "Two Carabinieri are a block away. They'll handle it."

Celeste Starr pushed her almost white blond hair over her shoulder and slipped her hand under her partner's arm. She and Brice Knox enjoyed keeping an eye on their Station Chief boss. *This is more exciting than being stuck in the office. Walk around and act like tourist.*

Brice unfolded a street map and walked a crooked path along the sidewalk. She remained at his side, holding his arm, and watching a short Arab beside a newsstand.

With his face buried in the map, Brice stumbled into a motorbike, knocking it off the stand. "Damn, my knee," he grabbed his leg and plopped on the overturned bike.

She leaned over him and slid a thin blade into the front tire. "Are you hurt?"

The Middle Eastern man ran to the motorbike and tried to lift it. Brice did not move as the man attempted to pull him off the bike.

"Move, that's my bike, I must leave."

Celeste seized his shirt and slung him aside. "Stop hitting him, he's hurt!"

Two Carabinieri, strolled toward the commotion.

Brice stood. The man pushed him and yelled. "Get out of my way."

The taller Carabiniere confronted him. "Leave that man alone." His deep voice startled people nearby, and they moved aside. He turned to Celeste.

"My name is Vincenzo. Is there a problem?"

"He assaulted my husband and shoved him into the motorbike. I heard him speak English," Celeste said.

Vincenzo glared at the man. "Why did you push him? These tourists are guests in my country."

The man replied in Arabic.

Vincenzo turned to his partner. "What did he say, Paolo?"

"I think it was no."

"No!" He glared at the man. "You think we're stupid? I saw you push him."

Again, the man muttered in Arabic.

"That time he said yes." Paolo said. "He confessed. If he has proper immigrant papers, I'll buy you dinner."

Vincenzo stepped close to the defiant Arab. "Give me your identification documents."

More Arabic mumbling.

Paolo smiled. "No, again. He said you're stupid."

Vincenzo spun the man around and clamped handcuffs to his wrist. "I think you better come with us." He held the short chain between the cuffs, looked at Celeste, and grinned. "I am sorry this happened while you are visiting my beautiful country."

She smiled and handed him a business card. "Thank you Vincenzo. We're staying at the Palace Royal Hotel, near the Spanish Steps."

Paolo nodded. "If we need more information someone will call. Enjoy your vacation in our Eternal City."

Josef pulled his Alfa Romeo into the stream of heavy traffic.

Al fidgeted with his seatbelt as both men fought to control their laughter.

"I almost laughed on our way to the car. The guy didn't know it was all a setup." Josef said.

"Laugh, I came close to pissing my pants."

Josef furrowed his brow and attempted to stop his smile. "Let's plan to go out for coffee again tomorrow."

"Stop it, please."

"You want to talk to him," Josef asked.

"Hell yes. If someone in Al Qaeda sent him, he may be loaded with information."

Josef grabbed his cell phone. "I'll find out where they're taking him."

XIII

IT'S OUR DUTY

Saleh and Zarina ate dinner at the dining room table.

Zarina pushed her food around her plate and took a deep breath. "How long will we stay here?"

Saleh stared at her and paused before he spoke. "Are you worried about our future?"

"This isn't the way we should live. I want things to be like they were."

"Before what? Before the children died, and the prophet sent me a message? Or before I told Akram I am finished killing for him?"

"Before all of it!"

"Please try to understand," he said setting his fork on his plate. "What I did was wrong. Nothing can be the same after my plan failed and killed those Muslim children."

Zarina threw her head back and locked her icy gaze on his eyes. "Muslims have struggled for centuries... why do you say it's wrong?"

"Tell me, Zarina. Why have we struggled for so long?"

"To bring Islam to the world."

Saleh nodded. "It's our duty, just as it's the duty of every religion to spread the word of their faith."

Zarina raised her eyebrows and smiled. "Then how can you say it's wrong?"

"It isn't wrong. Each day Muslims, Christians and Jews work hard to gather more followers."

"Saleh, you're making no sense."

He knew he could control the conversation. *She is smart, but a follower and thick headed.* He shook his head. "That's because you haven't heard what I've been saying." He reached to take her hand, but she slid it to her lap. "I watched those children die."

Her gaze bounced around the room and she pounded her small fist on the table. "It was an accident. Why can't you accept that?"

"No, it was a sign."

"What sign?" she yelled.

Finally. Once she became emotional, he could lead her around in circles by answering her question with a question. "How many people will follow Islam by force?"

"I don't know."

"How many of our Muslim brothers should we kill because they are not fundamentalist and follow the prophet's cousin?"

Zarina raised her voice. "I don't know." Tears formed.

"Would it be better to train children to be doctors... or Martyrs?"

"I don't know, Saleh!"

He slammed his hand on the table startling her. "Don't you understand? We kill people... then demand that those we allow to live respect us and honor our teachings. Is that the way to bring people to accept Islam?"

Zarina shoved her chair away from the table with such force it fell. "They must convert!"

Akram's cell phone sat on the table in front of him. He planted his elbows near it and listened to Gafar on the speaker.

"What is being done?" Gafar asked.

"Two men have crossed into Italy."

"Are they going to the house?"

Akram hesitated and looked at the ceiling. "Yes. First, they'll go to a garage we rented in a nearby town. A car and weapons are there. I told them to take whatever time is necessary."

"Did you explain to them that my daughter is with him?"

Akram shook his head. Their leaders didn't care about Gafar's daughter and neither did he. Saleh needed to die before he talked. *No reason to tell this Saudi my men plan to blow up the house.* "Yes, I did."

"Their lives depend on her not being hurt." Gafar said.

Angelo sat next to Joe in straight back chairs in front of Colonel Giuseppe Aldo's desk. He had warned his American partner before they arrived that the colonel was not in a good mood. Neither man moved nor diverted their eyes from their boss.

Aldo stared at them for a full fifteen seconds without blinking. "I like you Inspector Costa, your work has impressed me." His eyes moved to Angelo. "I gave you the job of organizing and running the Fugitive Task Force because of your skills and tenacity. I did not bring both of you here to threaten you, only to... as the American's say, light small fires under your asses." His eyes paused for a moment on each man. "How did he register in a hotel, in the middle of central Rome, without us knowing about it?"

"He and his wife registered with British passports," Angelo said.

Aldo looked around his office shaking his head. "This is not America, Angelo. People don't shoot automatic weapons on the streets of our cities."

"Yes, sir."

Aldo placed both arms on the desk and leaned forward. "You and Inspector Costa will be busy and lose a lot of sleep. I don't care what it takes. Find him before someone else dies."

"One of our agents will get lucky, sir." The moment the words came out of Angelo's mouth he realized his mistake.

Aldo glared at him. "Luck better have nothing to do with it, Captain Randi. Take him into custody before his Al Qaeda friends kill him."

Joe sat forward in his chair. "We now have three names he uses and a complete description of the car, including the tag number."

Aldo looked at Joe and raised his eyebrows. "I suggest you and Angelo go to church tonight and pray he doesn't have more names on different passports, or a second car."

"We'll find him, sir," Angelo said. "When we do, we have plans to make sure no one can get to him."

"First you need to get your hands on him. Both of you may want to light a candle before you pray. What can I do to help?" Aldo asked.

"We want to ask Witness Security in America for help. A request from someone with a little more influence than Angelo and me would get a quicker response," Joe said.

Aldo grinned. "I have the name of just the man. Now get to work."

Both men walked out and Joe cornered Angelo in the hallway outside the colonel's office. "I haven't been that uncomfortable in years."

Angelo took a deep breath and exhaled. "That was nothing. You should see him when he's angry."

Joe smiled. "Pick a nearby church and we'll go there now."

Ahmed and his brother Jafar each carried an RPG 7 rocket-propelled grenade launcher as they snaked their way down the hillside behind Musa's country villa. Both men wore tan clothing to blend in with the color of the ground on the hillside. They crouched and moved through the moonlit night seeking the best concealment in the trees and brush.

It had taken them less than twenty four hours to get into Italy, pick up the weapons and a car at a garage outside Rome.

When they reached a point fifty meters from the house. Ahmed raised his arm to stop Jafar. "Here, we're close enough. We'll wait until after midnight, they'll both be asleep." He raised a pair of binoculars.

Saleh leaned back on the couch and removed two British and two German passports from the briefcase, He looked at the photo on each document and stared at the floor. *How did they find us in Rome? Akram knows the car. That's it, the car.* He looked up and saw Zarina standing in the bedroom doorway watching him. "I think I know how they found us."

"What do you mean?"

"After I spoke with Akram, he must have had someone put a tracking device on the BMW. All he would need to do is turn on his computer and it would show our location. We may need to leave here, but we're safe for tonight. I'll check the car in the morning."

Zarina walked across the room. "Do you believe he would do that?"

"Yes. We're a threat to him, and his followers."

"Why don't you check it now?"

"No. There's not enough light."

"It's late, Saleh. Are you going to sleep tonight?"

He threw the passports into the briefcase and closed it.

"Will you change your mind and contact my father?"

"I want us to be free of all this. Calling your father isn't the answer."

"It's been our life for many years. We were happy."

At times during their marriage, Zarina played the part of a helpless wife to get her way. It may work with a stranger, but Saleh had seen her ploy too many times.

"Yes, but think. What life have we had? Going out to enjoy ourselves, without being cautious, is out of the question. Wouldn't you be happier with friends who did not look over their shoulders each time they go shopping?"

"It's always been this way. We've sacrificed our lives for our cause."

Saleh stood and pulled her to him. "It's time to think of ourselves and our future, not our past life." He looked into her eyes and thought about the many years of happiness they had shared. *I should have made this decision a long time ago.* "Come, we'll go to bed and talk about..."

An explosion ripped open a wall. The force of the blast, knocked them to the floor and filled the room with smoke, dust, and debris.

"Saleh!" Zarina screamed.

He looked toward the sound of her voice and saw his briefcase through the haze. He crawled toward it and saw Zarina, in a fetal position against the wall, her hands clamped over her ears. Saleh grabbed the briefcase and dragged it to her side. "Get up! We need to get out of this room." He pulled her to her feet and shoved her through the bedroom door just as a second explosion brought down a section of the ceiling and knocked them to the floor beside the bed.

XIV

DECISION TIME

Early the next morning, Saleh sat at the kitchen table and watched firefighters scurry from the section of the house destroyed by the explosions.

He looked at Zarina and saw a tear slide down her cheek. *If I'd stayed in Milan and waited for the police to check the name Halabi, I'd have more bargaining power. Why was I so stupid? His* eyes came to rest on the set of handcuffs attached to Zarina's right wrist and the chair. A handcuff, locked in the same fashion as hers, kept him from raising his left hand above waist level.

A police officer, with a red cross on his sleeve, bandaged minor cuts on their arms.

Saleh glanced at the huge officer guarding them from a position near the door and watched as a sergeant stepped into the room.

"Who are your important friends?" the sergeant asked.

Saleh glanced at his wife and turned to him. "What important friends?"

"The people who are keeping you out of jail."

Saleh shrugged. "I have no friends with that power."

The sergeant rolled his eyes. "Sure you don't. No one ever admits they have political connections." He shook his head on the way out of the room.

Zarina looked at Saleh and raised her eyebrows. "What did he mean?"

He focused on the center of the table. The only person he knew with political friends in Italy was Akram. The thought of the old man's reach, all the way from Iran, terrified him. A whisper into someone's ear and a thousand Euros in their pocket was all it would take. "If he meant Akram, we'll be dead before tomorrow night."

Three men in expensive looking suits walked into the room. Saleh's eyes locked on them. *Local police officers don't wear tailored suits. Who are they?*

The one with black hair and a goatee walked up and stood in front of him. "Should I call you Saleh al-Filistini or Mohammad Halabi?"

Saleh took a second before he replied. "al-Filistini."

"May I call you Saleh?"

Saleh nodded.

The man turned to Zarina and stared at her for a full five seconds. "And you, madam, are Zarina al-Ansari from Riyadh, Saudi Arabia?"

Her eyes widened, moved to Saleh and then back to the man. "Yes."

"May I call you Zarina?"

"Yes."

"I am Carabinieri Captain Angelo Randi." He had decided to keep everything as formal as possible for the time being and motioned to the young man beside him. "This is Inspector Gino Palma of the Italian State Police." He pointed to the third man. "Inspector Joe Costa from America's U.S. Marshals Service." He looked from Zarina to Saleh and paused. "Both of you are lucky, and Akram's men are incompetent."

Saleh hid his surprise by biting the inside of his cheek and saw Zarina stiffen. "I don't know anyone named Akram."

Angelo's eyes lingered on him and he smiled. "We did not come here to lie to you. A man in Rome told us a different story. He said you worked for Akram and were once good friends." He turned to Zarina. "Is that true Zarina?"

Saleh held his breath. *These men are not fools.* He glanced at Inspector Costa. *Why is an American here?* "My wife knows nothing of this."

"I doubt that," Angelo said. "We will discuss her future later. We came here today to spend only a short time with you. In the next few minutes, you will make a single decision."

"What if I'm unable?" Saleh asked.

"It should not be a problem, it's simple."

Saleh looked into Zarina's terror stricken eyes before turning to Angelo. "I may need to speak with my wife before I can give you an answer."

"Discussing it will not be necessary."

Saleh took his time digesting everything Angelo had said. His life was about to change but he couldn't be sure if it would be for the better.

Angelo leaned toward him. "Shall we meet tomorrow to discuss your future, or should I tell the officers outside to find you both accommodations in separate prisons?"

Zarina's body tensed. Her free hand clutched Saleh's arm, her eyes filled with tears, and focused on his face.

He looked at her small hand and covered it with his to calm her. "Are you saying you will not take us to jail?"

Angelo nodded. "Not today... and maybe not tomorrow. You will make that decision for me."

Saleh felt Zarina's hand squeeze his arm. "And after that?"

"Your future decisions determine what I will do. For now, you must decide on jail or limited freedom in comfortable surroundings."

"Where will you take us?" Zarina asked.

"You'll go to a house with my men."

Saleh glanced at Zarina and looked back at Angelo. "Where?"

"The location doesn't matter. It's a house where you'll be safe."

Saleh tilted his head and pressed his lips together. "Can we discuss..."

Angelo raised a hand to stop him. "I need your answer. Now."

Saleh rubbed his chin and stared at Angelo. "We'll go to the house. I think you and I have much more to discuss."

Angelo turned to the officer standing in the doorway. "Remove their handcuffs."

Early the next morning, Joe walked into his office at the U. S. Embassy and nodded to Gino Palma, leaning against the couch armrest. "Hi Gino."

A large plaque of a United States Marshals badge hung on the wall, and a carved wooden nameplate on the desk identified Joe Costa, Inspector, United States Marshals Service.

Joe took a seat in front of Gino. "Angelo's on his way."

"From what I've seen, Angelo's tough," Gino said. "I wouldn't want to make him my enemy, but al-Filistini may think he's important enough to push him around."

Joe grinned. "Behind his back we call him 'the bull', but I wouldn't say that to his face. He can handle Saleh. He'll play the guy like a church organ."

They heard a knock on the door and Angelo, in a Carabinieri uniform, entered.

"Good morning," Joe said.

Angelo nodded. "Gino... Joe."

Angelo sat beside Gino. "A few minutes ago I verified your government approved our request for assistance. Soon we'll see if your Witness Security Division will help us hide al-Filistini. Gino will handle the case in our Program."

"Who did you meet with?" Joe asked.

"The Deputy Chief of Mission and Al Provitti. The ambassador received the approval message an hour ago. Al said the intelligence community supported the request one hundred percent." He smiled. "Colonel Aldo agreed with our plan with one exception. He wants you to handle the American side of the case and not someone new from Witness Security. He wants no one else around Saleh and said your ten years' experience working the program is sufficient."

Joe pondered Angelo's words and was about to speak when he continued.

"The intelligence services realize Saleh is loaded with information and they want to get it. Everyone agreed he will be more comfortable in America, and much more willing to talk if he isn't locked down in an Italian safe house."

Joe shook his head. "There's one big problem. WITSEC is protective of their business. They won't welcome an outsider, even one with my experience, back into the fold as a part time Witness Security Specialist. They may not go along with it."

Angelo grinned. "Aldo made it clear. If they don't agree to let you handle the case, there will be no American involvement. He doesn't trust many people; you're one of the few."

Joe raised his eyebrows. "He told me he did, but I thought he was blowing smoke up my ass. I guess he was serious. I still need to contact my boss and have him speak to someone at the Justice Department."

Angelo laughed. "You're not listening to what I'm saying, Joe. Colonel Giuseppe Aldo gets what he wants. It will happen. You're supposed to get a call by five this afternoon."

Joe shook his head. *How powerful can Aldo be?* "The chief of WITSEC will be mad as hell."

"Maybe, but he'll hide it and walk around his headquarters with a smile on his face. The Minister of Foreign Affairs already called your Secretary of State."

Joe avoided the petty politics that worked their way down the ladder in every organization administered by a political appointee. *If Aldo made this happen at that level of our government, I won't have to worry about anyone screwing with me.*

Gino scooted to the edge of the couch. "When do you want us to explain our programs to him and his wife?" he asked Angelo.

"Today."

Joe nodded. "We'll need a few hours. Did you tell him it's voluntary?"

"Not yet. I don't think there will be a problem."

Joe shook his head. "He may refuse the program."

Angelo grinned and raised his eyebrows. "When I finish telling him about the prison he's going to, he'll agree. I've never taken you to visit any on them. Before this thing is over, I'll get you a private tour of San Vittore in Milan... built in 1880, and the Poggioreale in Naples... built in 1905."

"They still use them?"

Angelo nodded. "They've made a few upgrades but they're nothing like your country club penitentiaries."

XV

THE RATS OF POGGIOREALE

Saleh and Zarina sat close to each other on a love seat in a one-bedroom apartment with no windows and a solid metal entry door. He peered around the living room and stopped on the telephone on the end table next to him. *No numbers to dial... why is it here?*

They had arrived yesterday in a blacked out van and were blindfolded before they walked to the apartment. Once inside and free of the blindfolds, he saw the surprise on Zarina's face. It wasn't the worst place they'd stayed.

He and Zarina had taken their time and walked through each room. The bedroom had separate beds, the living room spacious, and the kitchen well stocked with dishes, pans and food. Two things bothered him. *There's no windows to look out, and I can't hear any sounds from beyond the walls.*

Zarina clutched her handbag and pulled it closer to her side. "This isn't a house."

Saleh nodded. "Whatever it is, it's secure."

"What do they want with..."

The telephone rang.

Saleh looked at her as he lifted the handset. "Yes." He whispered Angelo's name. "Yes, we are." He hung up the phone.

Both looked at the metal door when they heard a deadbolt turn.

Angelo stepped into the room and motioned to a chair. "May I?"

Saleh nodded. "Please."

He moved it closer to them, took a seat, and looked at Zarina. "You have a cell phone that does not work?"

"Yes." She removed a phone from her purse and handed it to him. "After my brother's murder, my husband told me to throw away the SIM card. I went to the bathroom and flushed it down the toilet."

Angelo slid open the back, examined the empty SIM card slot and returned the phone to Zarina. "Did you sleep well," he asked.

"No." Saleh said.

Angelo shrugged. "No view but it's much nicer than the Poggioreale Prison in Naples. For many years we tried to clean that place up, but the rats have been there longer than the Italian government."

Zarina glared at Saleh.

"These accommodations are comfortable," Saleh said.

Angelo smiled. "Good. Today you will need to make another decision about your future."

Saleh stared at the Carabinieri captain and pondered. Somehow, he needed to gain more control by bargaining with them. *They want information from me, but I want things from them.*

"If you and your wife wish to stay alive you will need the help of my government, and the government of the United States."

Zarina repositioned herself and crossed her arms. "What can the Americans do for us?"

"Along with Italy, provide for your safety. You should feel secure knowing two great countries will use their resources to make sure you continue to breathe fresh air. Your own people are trying to kill you. You know that don't you?"

Her jaw tightened, and she glared at Angelo. "What will you ask of us?"

"For now, Zarina, your responsibility is your husband's welfare, nothing more."

"And me?" Saleh asked.

"We want every piece of information you have in your head. You must agree to truthfully answer the questions of those we bring to interview you."

"Who?" he asked.

"A.I.S.E., the CIA and law enforcement."

Zarina's shoulders drooped. Saleh touched his temple and closed his eyes for a moment He opened them and stared at Angelo. "If we do what you ask, we'll be dead the next day."

"If we wanted you dead, you would be cell-mates with the rats in Naples."

Saleh took a deep breath and shook his head. "No one can insure our safety."

"The people who will help you are professionals. They can make you disappear and reappear as a married couple any place on earth." Angelo clasped his fingers together and studied his two captives for a few seconds. "Shall we begin so

I can make the appropriate arrangements, or would you like me to arrange transportation for you to Naples?"

Saleh pursed his lips. *This won't be easy.* He looked at Zarina, tilted his head, and turned to Angelo. "I need to speak with my wife."

Angelo stood and nodded. "If you agree, lift the telephone. Someone will answer and I will send in Inspector Palma and Inspector Costa to explain the arrangements. Please don't take long to decide." He crossed the room, pulled open the heavy door, and stepped out. The deadbolt snapped into place with a loud clank.

Zarina's hands trembled. "You can't do this. I don't trust them."

"What choice do we have?"

"They're asking you to betray our cause, our families."

Saleh took her hand. "If we go to prison, it will take Akram one day to have us killed. We need to listen to what they propose and decide what is best for us under these circumstances."

Joe and Gino sat in a room outside the secure apartment and watched Angelo pace the floor.

"Think he'll take the deal?" Joe asked.

Angelo stopped and smiled. "When I told him about the large rodents at the Poggioreale his wife didn't look happy. I thought she would vomit on the floor." He shrugged. "Naples has a problem with the garbage collector's union. It wouldn't surprise me if the rats paid union dues."

"That's the place you want me to visit?" Joe asked.

"It's one of the oldest prisons in Italy. The capacity is fourteen hundred, but in the past year the population rose to two thousand nine hundred. Most of the prisoners are locked in their cells for twenty-two hours a day."

Angelo's playing hardball, Joe thought. If that prison was any sign of what Saleh and his wife faced, he didn't doubt they'd agree. "I guess he..." His cell phone beeped, and he looked at the text message. "The Witness Security Division accepted the case. We leave in three days from Sicily."

Angelo smirked. "Talk to him. Make sure he accepts our offer. I'm going for coffee." He stopped at the door and looked at Joe. "I'm glad we have time to plan before we leave. Can you be in my office tomorrow afternoon at four?"

"Sure, is anything wrong?"

"No. A new development... slight change in our organizational structure."

Joe watched the door close and turned to Gino. "You'll be mad when you hear this." He continued reading the text message. "Approved, date and time follows. You and Captain Randi depart, on a C-141, out of Sigonella Naval Air Station in Sicily. Destination, MacDill Air Force Base, Tampa, Florida."

Gino stiffened in his chair. "What about me?"

"It's not all bad." Joe said and continued. "Inspector Palma will be the primary contact person in Italy. Arrangements will be made for his arrival at Marshals Service headquarters next month."

"A trip to Florida would have been better, but at least I'll get to see Washington," Gino said smiling. "Let's talk to them."

Saleh raced across the room to answer the ringing telephone. "Yes... Please come in."

Gino led Joe into the apartment. Both men held briefcases.

"Mr. al-Filistini, we met. I'm Inspector Gino Palma, and this is Inspector Joe Costa. We are both Witness Security

Specialists. Inspector Costa works for the American Department of Justice."

"Here in Italy?" Zarina asked.

Joe nodded. "Yes."

"We're here to answer your questions. If you agree to the terms of our programs, both of you are required to sign the documents." Gino said. "Shall we sit?"

Saleh pointed at a round table and four chairs near the kitchen.

Both Gino and Joe removed thick folders from their briefcases and dropped them on the table. Everyone took a seat.

"Before we talk about protection and services, there are things you should know," Gino said.

"Our programs are voluntary, both of you must agree to the rules," Joe said. "It is critical both of you understand that if you violate these rules you will be terminated from the programs, and protection will stop."

Saleh raised his eyebrows. "Terminated?"

Gino smiled. "It means removed from the program and nothing more."

"If my wife doesn't agree, can she return to Saudi Arabia?"

Gino shook his head. "That's not an option. We'll arrange for her to be moved to a jail and held to face charges in an Italian court."

Saleh glanced at Zarina. As far as he knew, they couldn't charge Zarina with anything. "What charges?"

"Suspicion of terror association and subversion. Ask Captain Randi for the details, he has photos that may explain our decision," Gino said.

Zarina's shoulders slumped forward. "Will I ever see my family again?"

"No." Gino said.

She shook her head and stared at the ceiling. Tears rolled down her cheeks.

Saleh took his wife's hand. "I have money in a bank account."

Joe raised his head. "Where?"

Saleh hesitated. *They'll take it... no, they don't know the name.* "Zurich."

"How much?" Gino asked.

"Almost a million Euros."

Neither of the investigators reacted. "Ask Angelo. He has friends who can help you securely transfer the money," Gino said.

Saleh glanced at Zarina's trembling hands on her lap.

"Will I have to testify?" he asked Joe.

"That's up to government officials in America and Italy. The aspects of your criminal case are not the concern of witness security."

"Our role is to keep you alive, move you to a safe place, establish your new identity, and help you assimilate into a community." Gino said. "Testimony is not a requirement for protection. Let's begin."

Saleh noticed Zarina looking around the room. "Is something wrong?"

Zarina paused and stared at him with her mouth open. "No. We must do as they ask." She nodded to Gino. "Continue."

"The first thing we'll discuss is your need to follow our instructions and abide by the rules we will explain to you." Joe said. "Without your complete cooperation, we cannot keep you alive."

###

Three hours later, Gino, Joe, and Angelo, in a room outside the apartment, leafed through papers scattered across the table.

"Good," Angelo said.

"Everything is arranged. Witness Security in Italy and the U.S. will make all the decisions," Joe said.

"How many people will know where they are living," Angelo asked.

"Besides us; Aldo, the Chief of WITSEC, and one Case Analyst. Gino shouldn't need to bring in anyone else unless they're moved back to Italy." Joe grinned. "I guess the three of us make the decisions."

Angelo squinted and furrowed his brow. "There's one thing that's bothering me. So far, his friends haven't had a difficult time finding him. They tried to kill him twice in Rome and once at the villa. He's lucky to be alive."

Gino smiled. "It's like he has a GPS implanted in his ass."

XVI

YOU NEED HELP

The next day, Joe walked into Angelo's outer office at five minutes to four and stopped. *What does he have up his sleeve?* He had hoped he would run into Mia, but her chair was empty. The door to Angelo's office stood open. "Angelo?"

"Come in."

Angelo met him halfway across the room, pointed at the chairs near the low table, and both sat. "You need to go back to the embassy today?"

"No. Why all the secrecy?"

Angelo took a deep breath. "I consider you a close friend. We've worked together for ten months and I think of you a member of my family. My wife and Mia both like you."

Joe leaned back and stared at his partner. "Okay. What did I do wrong?"

"Nothing. We've built a great organization together, and we arrested some of Italy's most wanted fugitives."

Angelo doesn't beat around the bush, something's up, and it's important to him. Joe couldn't remember the last time Angelo made such a request. Clearing his late afternoon schedule wasn't surprising, but a little out of the ordinary. Whatever it was, Joe wanted it settled, now.

"Come on, Angelo, I know that. Why are you stalling? Something happened and I want to know about it."

Mia called through the doorway that she had returned.

Angelo raised his voice. "Thank you, Mia." He leaned toward Joe. "You can tell I've been delaying?"

"Of course I can. It's not like you. Get to the point. I can take it."

"Okay. I've decided to bring in another person."

Joe shook his head. *It makes little sense.* Law enforcement agencies in the States didn't like to share information, but the Italians were notorious for interagency rivalry and case secrecy. *Got to be someone from within the Carabinieri.* "This is crazy. You and I have done everything together with no one's help for almost a year... why now? Aren't you satisfied with the job I'm doing?"

"Yes, I'm satisfied. No one could do it better. If your government tries to transfer you back to America, I'll fight them."

"Come on, Angelo. Why the hell do we need help?"

Angelo sighed and filled his lungs. "Well, we don't need help, you do."

"Me! I'm the guy who drew up the organizational structure and presented the plan to Colonel Aldo."

"I know, and Aldo said if he has anything to do with it, you'll spend the rest of your career here in Italy." He called to the open door. "Mia, bring us coffee."

Joe's muscles tensed. "We're leaving for Sicily tomorrow. I don't know if I have enough time to make arrangements for another person on the plane."

"Everything will fall into place. It won't be a problem," Angelo said.

"Listen, it takes time to build trust." Joe shook his head. "You can't just bring someone in. It will take months to learn our procedures and be accepted by the guys working the streets. I don't like this... I'm doing fine and everything is going..."

Angelo held up his hand to stop him. "Please Joe. Soon you'll be doing better."

"Better than what? There's nothing wrong with me."

Mia walked through the doorway empty handed and Angelo stood.

Joe looked at him as if he were crazy. *What the hell is he doing? Since when does he stand for Mia?*

Joe followed suit.

A tall young woman in form-fitting black low cut jeans, red heels and a red silk blouse stepped into the office carrying a tray with four espresso cups. Joe's mouth dropped open. Her long brown hair flowed over her shoulders and down her back. She set the tray on the table and stepped in front of Joe. He stared into her blue-gray eyes and didn't blink until she kissed him on both cheeks.

"Hi, Joe. I'm Nina, Sofia's cousin."

He closed his mouth and smiled. Angelo had told him she was pretty, but stunning was the word he should have used. Rome was known for its beautiful high-fashion women, but until this moment, none had grabbed his attention like the gorgeous lady inches in front of him. For a split second, time stopped and his broad smile lit the room. "Nice to meet you, Nina." He motioned to his partner. "Angelo said you were in London. He's been hiding you from me."

"My transfer to Rome was approved."

Joe looked at his partner and raised his eyebrows. "We're leaving tomorrow. Why didn't you tell me sooner?"

Nina answered before he could speak. "I arrived last night."

"I made reservations for dinner at seven," Angelo said. "Sofia cannot join us so Mia agreed to be my date for the evening."

Joe glanced at Angelo. "I've got nothing planned for the rest of the day or tonight." He looked at the two women. "Angelo and I may have to fight off the crowd. Every man in Rome will be jealous."

For the next two and a half hours, he seldom took his eyes off Nina, except to grin at the equally beautiful Mia, or glance at Angelo. They discussed Nina's job with Alitalia Airlines, Joe's family in Italy, and the places they both liked and could visit together when he and Angelo returned to Italy. He wanted to grab her and tell her he'd cancel his trip. *Play it cool, be calm, and pray she doesn't meet someone.*

That night, Angelo and Mia left the restaurant at half past ten. Joe and Nina shared another bottle of wine.

XVII

A NEW BEGINNING

At eight PM, the corporate jet pulled into a private hanger at Atlanta's Hartsfield-Jackson International Airport, and shut down its engines beside a black SUV with dark tinted windows. The door opened and stairway deployed.

Joe, in slacks and a sport shirt, carried a suitcase as he descended the steps, and headed to the SUV. *Sicily to Atlanta via Tampa. Thank God twenty one hours traveling from Italy has ended.* He removed the keys from the ignition, opened the rear hatch, and threw his suitcase in the back.

Angelo passed him luggage from the plane and stepped aside, allowing Saleh and Zarina access to the exit.

Joe stretched his back and legs, then loaded their bags into the SUV. He walked to the side of the vehicle, leaned across the steering wheel, and turned on the engine and air conditioner. "Everyone is stiff from small airplane seats," he said to Saleh. "Walk around for a few minutes and then we'll leave."

Angelo bent forward stretching and reaching for his ankles. "Now I know why I didn't join the Air Force." He looked around the hanger. "It would have been nice to stay in Florida."

Joe shrugged. "MacDill Air Force Base was where the plane from Sicily was going. WITSEC headquarters wanted us to come to Atlanta."

The SUV pulled onto the highway near the airport. Joe glanced at Saleh in the rearview mirror. "Tired?"

"Yes."

"Where are we?" Zarina asked.

"Atlanta, Georgia, the southeastern part of the country."

"Where are you taking us?" Saleh asked.

Joe opened the center console and removed a brochure and a key card. "A hotel room, about thirty minutes from here."

"How long will we stay there?" Zarina asked.

"One night, tomorrow you'll move to a furnished apartment."

Saleh leaned between the two front seats. "Will the police guard us?"

Angelo turned to him. "You're safe here... there's no need for guards."

Joe noticed Zarina frown at Saleh. *Culture shock.*

She glanced out the window at the large cars on the highway, the skyscrapers in downtown Atlanta, and then back at Saleh.

"Must we stay in the room... can we go out?" Saleh asked.

"There's no need to hide," Joe said. "But don't go too far. You have no identification."

"How can we leave the room? We need documents," Zarina said.

Angelo looked at her. "America is not like Europe. No one will ask you to identify yourself. The hotels don't even record your personal information and notify the police when you register."

Joe raised a hand from the wheel. "Remember Al Provitti? He's making arrangements for temporary identification documents." He handed Saleh a folded paper. "You're registered as Saleh and Zarina Sania. It's written on the paper. Practice using that name. I wrote my cell phone number on the page. If it's important, call me."

Angelo looked back. "Never use the name al-Filistini again."

"Why have you done this?" Zarina shouted.

"What?" Joe asked.

"Given us the same name. I have my own name, Zarina Gafar Muhammad al-Ansari!"

Joe glared at her in the rearview mirror. "I know it's customary for you to keep your own name. Here, most women take their husbands name after marriage. Someone in Washington picked Sania... it's temporary. When your new legal name is chosen you can pick something different than your husband... so long as it's not associated with the Ansari family or any of their friends."

Zarina focused on Joe's eyes in the mirror. "You should have thought of this."

"Maybe, but we didn't. Try to relax and not make life more difficult."

"You trust us to be alone?" Saleh asked.

"Yes. You signed an agreement. Violate it and you'll be returned to Italy and sent to prison," Angelo said.

Joe glanced over his shoulder. "No one will ask you for identification unless you do something stupid. Since you'll be at the hotel for only one night, it's best if you eat at their restaurant or one nearby. Please don't think about fleeing. If, by chance, you cross into Canada or Mexico, they'll hold you until you're identified. When they do, we'll come to pick you up and as Angelo said, you'll be returned to Italy and sent to prison."

Joe pointed at an exit from the highway. "We're almost there." He pulled into a parking lot in front of a multi-story Embassy Suites, drove to the side entrance and parked.

An hour later, Saleh and Zarina sat at a small kitchenette table in a two-room suite. Five, ten, and twenty dollar bills lay in front of them.

Zarina scanned the room, looked at the money and sighed. "How much did he give you?"

"Three hundred dollars."

"How can we live?"

"Three hundred for today, and tomorrow." From the moment he made his decision, he knew Zarina would oppose it. With each new confrontation, his patience diminished. *Stay calm. It'll take time for her to adjust.*

"Are you happy with what you've done?" she said, looking at the money on the table.

"What do you mean?"

"I can never go back to Saudi Arabia."

Saleh shook his head. "There's no reason to return."

"I'll never see my family again."

"Your place is with me. We can build a new life together."

"I love you Saleh, but you ask too much."

"The Americans and Italians will not allow you to return to Riyadh." he said.

"I would go without them knowing. You are the one who thinks the Prophet sent a message."

"You have no documentation. How can you leave?"

Zarina looked at her fingers, picked at one of her nails and did not answer.

"You're my wife, stand beside me. We're here for one day. Tomorrow we'll move into someplace larger."

"I don't like it... but I will." She shoved her chair from the table and stormed to the bedroom.

The day after they moved into their new apartment, Saleh noticed Zarina pouting. She spent thirty minutes pacing from the kitchen, past the dining room table, into the living room and on to the two bathrooms. She surveyed each room with the intensity of a woman looking for her lost diamond ring.

He stood near the sliding glass doors to a spacious balcony and watched her curl up on the couch pressing her handbag against her leg and the armrest. "Do you like the apartment?"

"It's okay." She did not look at him.

"It's better than the one in Italy."

She ignored his words. "What time are they taking us shopping?"

"They'll be here in an hour."

She continued to avoid looking in his direction. "How long will we stay here?"

"We have a new life, maybe a long time."

Zarina turned to him. "When will we get our money?"

He sighed and stepped in front of her. "I told you, Mr. Provitti said he would take care of it. It takes time to move that much money from one account to another."

Her face contorted and words hissed from her lips. "The CIA."

Saleh sighed. "The Americans will be honest."

"They're stupid. That's the reason they'll be defeated."

His hands closed to fists, and he exhaled. *Not again Zarina. Will you ever learn?* "Defeated... how? You think we can kill all of them?"

"If it takes a hundred years... our people immigrate, we'll conquer them. All infidels will turn to Islam."

Saleh nodded. "And if they don't?"

"Serve the needs of Islam or die."

He tried to suppress a laugh. "You don't understand America. You've lived in countries that are different... even repressive."

"How?"

"It's called freedom. People here treasure freedom."

She sat erect. "People in Saudi Arabia are free."

Saleh looked at her and rolled his eyes. "Are women allowed to drive cars on the streets of Riyadh?"

"No but..."

"Can they leave their homes alone to go shopping?" He didn't enjoy making his wife look foolish, but she needed to face the truth. In many countries of the Middle East women lived behind closed doors and did what men told them to do. *Is that what she wants?*

Zarina locked her eyes on his and tightened her jaw. "The Koran says..."

"How many Christian churches are in Saudi Arabia?"

She glared at him and pursed her lips. "None."

"In Europe did you have to carry a national identification card?"

"Yes!"

Saleh marched back to the sliding doors and pointed out the glass. "People out there don't carry cards to prove their citizenship." He turned to her. "In the west churches, synagogues and mosques exist on the same street. People of different religions pass each other on their way to pray."

She raised her voice and her nostrils flared. "Their beliefs violate the teachings of the Prophet."

Saleh shook his head and raised both hands. "So, because of beliefs... what they think... we should force them to submit or kill them?"

Zarina's dark eyes burned into him.

"After we kill a thousand, are we to smile at those who remain alive, and ask them to convert to Islam?" he asked. "Our friends kill people and sneak out the back door to slaughter Muslims in the marketplace because their prayers are different... women and children included. Maybe this is what you want Zarina." He slapped his chest. "But not me. I will not stand in the shadows and watch men enrich themselves by picking passages from the Koran and preaching hate to their followers."

Zarina grabbed her handbag and sprang from the couch. "I'm going to bathe."

Later that afternoon, Saleh and Zarina strolled through a mall with Joe and Angelo.

Joe stopped in front of a store. "I'll be back in a second." He headed through the door.

"He said it is going to rain," Angelo said.

Joe returned carrying two golf umbrellas, both with pointed four inch metal tips. He handed them to Saleh. "You'll need these later today. They're the biggest I could find... they'll keep you dry."

"Thank you," he handed one to his wife.

They sauntered past stores, stopping at displays to window shop.

Ahead of the group, a Muslim couple walked out of a store and stopped at the next display. The woman wore an abaya and hijab.

Zarina slowed, glanced at Saleh, raised her eyebrows and stopped. "Let's go the other way."

"Why?"

Her eyes darted to the woman. "Those people are Muslim," she said as the couple entered the store.

"There's many Muslims in America. They don't know you," Angelo said.

"A few months ago I came here with my brother," Joe said. "He bought a table in that store. I think the owner said he was from Damascus. Come."

Saleh took his wife's hand. "It's not a problem," he said.

The group headed toward the store.

"If they ask, tell them you're visiting from England," Joe said.

When they reached the entrance, Angelo stopped. "I'll wait here."

Saleh handed him the two umbrellas, and they walked into the store with Joe.

Joe noticed the Muslim couple speaking with a man he recognized. The man walked to Saleh.

"Hello, I'm Hami. Can I help you find something?"

Zarina slipped behind her husband and lowered her head.

"No, we're just looking," he said.

Hami studied him for a moment. "Are you Syrian?"

"No, English, but my mother is Lebanese. We're visiting from London."

Hami looked at Joe and furrowed his brow. "Have I seen you in my store?"

"Yes, two months ago. I thought I'd show my friends what you sold."

Hami nodded and smiled. He looked at Saleh and swept a hand toward items around the store. "If I can help you, please ask. I import from all over the Middle East."

"Thank you."

Hami returned to the Muslim couple. They glanced at Saleh and Zarina. The man nodded.

Zarina clutched Saleh's hand and lowered her voice. "Please Saleh, let's leave."

She's frightened, Joe thought.

"Okay." Saleh led them out of the store.

As they retraced their path through the mall, she kept glancing over her shoulder. "Joe, I want to leave."

Saleh placed his hand on her shoulder. "Is something wrong?"

"I'm scared."

Joe stepped beside them and nodded. "It takes time to adjust to a new environment. We'll take you back to the apartment."

As they approached Joe's SUV, Angelo turned to Zarina. "Tomorrow morning we'll come by to get Saleh. He needs to sign papers. You can go with us."

"I'll stay at the apartment."

"We won't keep him long," Joe said.

XVIII

THE CONFRONTATION

Gafar and Akram drank coffee at a small table in Akram's office.

"How old is the message?" Akram asked.

"One day. America makes it more difficult."

Akram furrowed his brow. "Saleh is important to them. Do you know where?"

"All I know is Atlanta, Georgia."

Akram pressed his lips together. "Florida is to the south. The sheik has friends there."

Gafar removed a paper from his pocket and unfolded it. "A contact in Rome said Saleh met with an American named Provitti. Someone told him he works at the U. S. Embassy."

Akram nodded and smiled. "This man may know where they are living. We need to search his house."

Don't be a fool, old man, Gafar thought. Akram often spoke before he engaged his brain. If the man worked at the American embassy, he'd be well protected. "More of your men will die, or they will kill innocent Italians, making our job difficult. Do nothing and wait. I'm sure we'll get more information."

Noon, the next day, the black SUV pulled to the entrance of the apartment building. Saleh opened the back door and stepped into a puddle. He looked at the clouds and the wet pavement from the recent rain as he grabbed his umbrella from the seat.

Joe lowered the window. "Tell your wife we said hello. If you need anything call me."

"Will you come tomorrow?"

Angelo leaned over to look at him. "After lunch, about two."

"Call first." He tapped the metal point of the umbrella against the pavement as he strode through the entrance, entered the elevator and pressed a button.

When the elevator door opened, he strolled to his apartment, reached for the doorknob and froze at the sound of a voice.

He placed his ear against the door and listened. After ten seconds, he unlocked the door and pushed it open.

Once inside, he heard Zarina speaking Arabic. He leaned the umbrella against the wall and tiptoed toward the sound of her voice. Outside the kitchen doorway, he pressed himself against the wall and strained to eavesdrop on her conversation. *She shouldn't be speaking Arabic to anyone. She can't be on a phone.* The muscles throughout his body tensed and his hands clenched when he stepped into the kitchen.

Zarina, facing away from him, held a red cell phone to her ear. His heart pounded as he glanced at a wooden block holding a set of kitchen knives and then focused on the phone.

"Who are you speaking with?"

Zarina jumped and spun toward him. With a terrified expression and taut lips, she fumbled to end the call.

"You were speaking Arabic!"

"I didn't... no I wasn't." Her gaze bounced around the room, avoiding direct eye contact.

"I remember you telling Angelo that phone didn't work."

She looked at the counter behind her and stepped back, pressing herself against the granite. "I lied."

Saleh glared at her and held out his hand. "Give me the phone."

"No."

He moved toward her.

Zarina threw the phone at him.

It bounced off his chest and clattered to the floor. He picked it up and stepped in front of her. "Who did you call?"

She stared at him in silence, her eyes burning into his.

He slammed his free hand across her cheek. The force of the blow knocked her against the counter. She steadied herself, wiped blood from the corner of her mouth, and pressed her hand against the side of her face.

"Answer me," he screamed.

Tears filled her eyes, and she glanced over her shoulder.

Nowhere to go, Zarina. He struck her face a second time with the back of his hand.

She leaned over the counter and sobbed, touching her split lip. Blood dropped to the granite.

Saleh raised the cell phone, tapped the screen and read the number. "This is your father's number. You've been telling him where we are. You're the one who wants me dead."

Zarina pushed herself up and glared at him. "I won't let you destroy my life!"

"You're a vicious woman, Zarina." He headed to the front door, picked up the umbrella, and looked at her standing in the kitchen doorway with a hand behind her back. "I should have left you in Italy and told the Italian authorities about your family."

"Where are you going?" she yelled.

"I don't want to see you again. I'm finished with you."

"Saleh, I'll find you. I'll kill you!"

The moment the words passed her lips, calmness came over Saleh. He thought about the shooting at the hotel, the explosives in the motorbike, and the rockets that almost killed him in the villa. "You and your father's friends tried three times and I'm still alive. You're nothing but a failure, Zarina."

"I will not fail. You will die!"

"Maybe I will, but I'll be alone and you will not see it happen. Now go back to your home. Go back to your friends who kill Muslim men, woman, and children for no reason except to control those they allow to live."

"No!" Zarina swung a large butcher knife from behind her back and leapt toward him.

With both hands he lifted the umbrella, the only thing he had to protect himself, and thrust the pointed metal tip into her chest.

Her eyes widened, face contorted, and she gasped. The knife dropped from her hand.

Saleh focused on the middle of her chest. He shoved the tip further into her body, leaned in and stared into her large eyes. "You failed again Zarina... your last failure." He loosened his grip as she slumped to the floor.

XIX

SHE IS DEAD

Joe and Angelo took their time driving along the two-lane country road back to his temporary office.

"Did you thank your brother for me?" Angelo asked.

"Yeah. He said he won't be back for two months. The house is ours... if we need it that long."

"If we're lucky, we'll be gone long before he returns." Angelo shook his head. "I feel sorry for Saleh, she's a bitch."

"She can be, but she's upset because she won't see her family again."

"During the trip over here, she kept her finger in his face and the complaining never stopped."

Joe shrugged. On the plane out of Sicily he spent most of his time talking with the crew and pilots. Ten years in WITSEC taught him two important lessons. He looked at Angelo "I learned two things working witnesses. Don't get too friendly with them. They're snitching on their friends and family and would like nothing more than to get something on you. Always remember, most of them are psychopaths. What you and I want doesn't matter, it's all about them. On the plane, I didn't pay them much attention. What's her complaint?"

"Money and family."

Joe nodded. He had heard the same story a hundred times. Everyone wanted the government to hand over the stolen money they squirreled away and then demanded the IRS not be informed. "She signed the agreement... may as well forget about family."

"When Provitti empties the account, maybe she will."

Joe laughed. "Amazing what a million will do."

Angelo nodded. "Have you talked to Nina?"

"Yeah, last night."

"She told me she likes you."

"The feeling is mutual. We're planning to take time off together when you and I get back to Italy." He smiled. "I thought someone that beautiful would be married."

"Nina is choosey and doesn't like to be told what to do."

"The only order I'd ever give her is to kiss me." His cell phone rang. "Hello." As he listened, he sat up in his seat. "Sure, is there a problem?" His muscles tightened. "What is it... are you all right?" The next words out of his phone made him cringe. He slammed on the brakes. "Dead!"

Angelo thrust his arms forward as the seat belt halted his flight into the windshield.

"We'll be there in a few minutes, don't do anything."

"What the hell happened?" Angelo repositioned himself.

Joe threw the SUV into a U-turn and smashed the accelerator to the floor. "Grab the blue light and plug it in here." He pointed to the empty cigarette lighter receptacle. Angelo handed him the flashing strobe light, and he rolled down his window and placed it on the roof. "He said Zarina is dead!"

Angelo's mouth dropped open, and he turned sideways. "Dead?"

Joe kept the SUV in the center of the lightly travelled road.

"I can't believe they found him," Angelo yelled. "How the hell are they tracking him and why would they kill her and not him?"

Joe looked at him. "You think he's calling them and trying to talk his way back into the organization? Even here, with the right contacts and a few hundred dollars, they'd be able to trace the phone calls."

Angelo focused on the dashboard before he replied. "Al Qaeda tried to kill him three times. I don't think he's that stupid."

"I don't know, but the first witness killed will not be on my watch."

He stopped along the curb in front of the apartment building and pulled the light from the roof. "Unplug it."

Joe looked at the building entrance and saw Saleh through the glass door. Both men jumped out and raced to him.

Joe looked at Saleh, then to Angelo and back at Selah. *How can this guy be so calm?*

"She's upstairs," Saleh said. He stepped into a stairway and took two steps at a time. Joe and Angelo scrambled to follow.

The three men entered a hallway, and Saleh led them to his apartment. He reached for the doorknob.

"Saleh!" Joe said stopping him from turning the knob. "We'll go in first. Is the door locked?"

"No."

Joe removed a Glock 27 from under his shirt and Angelo slid a Beretta PX4 Storm from his back waistband.

Joe's eyes widened. "What the hell! You're not supposed to have that."

Angelo shrugged. "I know, but I don't want to send you in there alone."

The day they departed Italy, a request went to the Department of Justice to get Angelo sworn in as a Special Deputy U. S. Marshal so he could carry a weapon. Joe hadn't received a reply and didn't know Angelo brought his weapon with him. *Screw it. One gun may not be enough.*

Saleh raised a hand. "You won't need those. No one is here."

Joe listened to his words, but it took a second for them to sink into his brain. *Better safe than sorry.* He cracked open the door, cradled the pistol with two hands, and shoved the door open with his foot. He and Angelo slipped into the apartment.

Zarina's crumpled body lay in a pool of blood, the long point of the umbrella buried in her chest.

Angelo raised his pistol to cover the inside of the apartment as Joe leaned over Zarina and checked for a pulse.

"She's dead, don't move anything," Joe said.

"Christ. How did this happen?" Angelo asked.

Saleh walked in and pointed at the knife lying on the floor beside her body. "I killed her because she tried to kill me."

Joe sucked air into his lungs and swung his head toward him. "You what?"

XX

THE TERRORIST FAMILY

Saleh sat on the couch and watched Joe and Angelo, both seemingly in a daze as they dropped into chairs. *There's no reason to continue protecting her.* He removed Zarina's cellular telephone from his pocket and handed it to Joe. "She told Angelo it didn't have a SIM card but it does. She's been calling her father and telling him where we were."

Angelo nodded. "I checked the phone when we first met. I should have done more, but she convinced me she threw it away."

Joe cocked his head, looked at Saleh and frowned. "Why haven't you told us anything about her father?"

"I loved her and didn't want to hurt her by telling you about him and his family."

Joe took his cell phone from his pocket and headed across the room. "I need to call Washington."

"We're not getting any sleep tonight," Angelo said. "Why would her father try to kill both of you?"

"He wouldn't. It's me he wants dead."

"Why?"

"The photos you have, don't tell the whole story. Zarina was a terrorist, everyone in her family is a terrorist." He rubbed his temple. "Do you know of Saudi Prince Mohammed bin Naif?"

"Sure," Angelo said. "The prince that's been a thorn in Al Qaeda's side for many years."

"We tried to assassinate him in 2009."

Angelo sat up and raised his eyebrows. "The body cavity bomber?"

"Yes, Abdullah Hassan al-Asiri. That was Zarina's idea... her plan."

Angelo swallowed hard and shook his head. "The only thing that saved the prince, was the short wall in front of him, and the fact that the bomb exploded inside Abdullah's body."

Joe ended his call and joined them. "An Assistant U.S. Attorney and someone from the U.S. Marshals office will be here soon."

Angelo bit his lower lip and scanned the room. "You need to call the local police?"

"Yeah, but not yet," Joe said.

Saleh glanced around the room. He had avoided jail up to now, but realized it may not be for long. *Surely they will understand, it was self-defense. I'm the one who can tell them everything.* "What will happen to me?"

Joe shrugged. "I can't answer that, but you'll remain protected."

"Will the police arrest him?" Angelo asked.

"It's up to them. The Associate Director told me he would ask the Attorney General's office to get involved."

"What about the press?" Angelo asked.

"A local Marshal will notify the police in person... too many people monitor their frequency."

Angelo leaned forward. "Saleh said Zarina's father is the one who's been trying to kill him."

Joe stared at Saleh for five full seconds. "Why the hell would he do that?"

Saleh hesitated, wondering how to word his next statement. With Zarina gone, he had no reason to continue hiding who she was. *Time to be honest.* "His daughter, Zarina's sister, was one of bin Laden's wives."

Joe pressed his fingers against his forehead. "Jesus, I better make another call." He walked to the kitchen.

Angelo scrambled to pull his cell phone from his pocket. "I'm calling Rome. After they find out bin-Laden was her brother-in-law, no one's ass will get much sleep."

Two hours later, Joe and Angelo had no more calls to make. Both sat with Saleh in the living room.

"All we can do now is wait for the big guns to arrive," Joe said. *What's taking them so long?*

There was a knock on the door and Joe checked the credentials of Chief Deputy Larry Gunn, from the local U.S. Marshals office, and Chief Assistant U.S. Attorney Maggie Hanover. He let them into the apartment.

Larry did not react when he stepped around Zarina's body but Maggie's eyes widened and she cringed.

"The Deputy Attorney General asked me to keep him apprised of the situation," Maggie said.

Joe nodded. "This is my partner, Italian Carabinieri Captain Angelo Randi, and Mr. Saleh Al-Sania, the dead woman's husband." He looked at Angelo. "This is Chief Larry Gunn and U. S. Attorney Maggie Hanover."

Maggie nodded, dragged a chair from the dining room and sat. Everyone stared at each other for a moment.

"WITSEC Chief Inspector Ralph Newberry should be here in a few minutes," Joe said.

"I heard you're not WITSEC," Larry said.

"No, fugitive investigations... assigned to the embassy in Rome."

"I guess that's why Newberry is on his way?"

"Everyone's got an ass to cover," Joe said.

Larry shook his head and looked at Joe. "Talking about ass cover, the Marshal is pissed. He wants to know why you chose his district as the relocation area."

"We'd rather keep politics out of this, Chief. I'm sure he wants to be reappointed... best if he gets his questions answered by headquarters." Joe glanced at Maggie and then back to Larry. "Were both of you told this case has national security ramifications?"

"Yeah, but that's about it," Maggie said.

"Did you call the locals?" Joe asked Larry.

"I contacted the Deputy Director at GBI, he's a friend. He sent one of his men to pick the Atlanta Deputy Chief of Criminal Investigations... they're friends. I didn't dare call anyone I couldn't trust."

"GBI?" Angelo asked.

"Georgia Bureau of Investigation," Joe said.

Maggie looked at Saleh. "Mr. Al-Sania, would you mind waiting in the bedroom? I don't want you to worry. The Attorney General of the United States assured me you'll be protected."

Saleh pushed himself from the couch. "Thank you." He left the room.

Maggie waited for the door to close and turned to Joe. "I don't know what this guy did. But based on his Arabic name, and the fact that I'm sitting here with an American investigator who works in Rome, and Carabinieri Captain Randi, it doesn't take a Rhodes Scholar to figure it out. In my twenty-two years with the U.S. Attorney's office, I never received a call from the number two at Justice. When he said the President wants this kept quiet, I almost fell out of my chair."

"We better come up with a good story about who this guy is, and what happened." Larry said.

Joe leaned forward. "I've got an idea that retains part of the truth, but someone will need to convince the locals."

"We'll leave that to the Attorney General's office," Maggie said. "When the locals arrive, I'll get him or an assistant on the phone. It's best if one person does the lying."

XXI

THE RAIDS

Five days after Zarina's death, Joe, Angelo, Saleh and FBI Terrorist Task Force Agent Zeller, sat at a conference table stacked with files and papers. Saleh had not held back any information. He answered every question Zeller asked.

On their way to the meeting, Joe agonized over how productive the interview would be. Now he sat across from the middle-aged agent and thanked God he wasn't at a table with Duffy or even worse, his bigger than life uncle. *Zeller's professional and attentive to every detail.*

Zeller shoved a stack of folders aside. "That's it. Not including the Middle East, we've covered seven countries. We'll take up the Arab countries the next time we meet."

Saleh nodded. "I already talked to Mr. Alfano and Mr. Provitti about them."

"I know," Zeller said. "We'll want to get more specific information... addresses, places they travel to and family member's locations."

Saleh cocked his head and paused. "Will you be able to arrest them in their countries?"

Zeller smiled. "No, but we can make their lives difficult. Let's see what we can do in the next few days, with the information you gave us."

Joe, Angelo, and Saleh stood.

Saleh extended his hand to Zeller. "Thank you... tell them to be careful. Al Qaeda is prepared."

Zeller nodded. "Joe, can I have a word with you?"

"Sure."

Angelo and Saleh left the room.

Zeller cocked his head. "His information damn well better check out. Do you trust him?"

Joe paused and stared at the FBI agent He trusted his mother. Others followed in a specific order, starting with Angelo and the Pope. He raised his head and rubbed his chin, but could not think of anyone else to add to the list. "Trust leads to betrayal. Betrayal leads to murder, or at least a good ass whipping out at the woodshed. I'm cautious. This guy has lost everything, including his wife. What would he gain by lying at this point?"

"Do me a favor," Zeller said. "Watch him until I let you know the operations in the next few days are completed. I don't want him making any phone calls."

Joe smiled. "I think his heart is in the right place. What's in his head? Self-preservation, rules. Don't worry, I've got it covered."

Special Agent King had spent three hours briefing his men. He now led five other FBI SWAT team members to a door on the fifth floor of a New York City apartment building on East 131st Street, in Harlem. A day earlier, he received information about two men, who crossed into Europe as refugees from Syria, and rented the apartment when they arrived six months ago from Munich, Germany. Intelligence officials identified them as members of a radical group operating in Iraq.

Each of King's man wore black tactical gear and held an MP5, 9mm submachine gun. Three men slipped to each side of the entrance. *No knocking to announce ourselves on this one.* One man held a door ram.

King nodded and whispered. "Now."

The agent stepped in front of the door, slammed the blunt end of the ram into the metal near the deadbolt and stepped out of the way.

A man from the other side of the entrance threw his shoulder against the door near the bent lock, and burst into the apartment screaming. "FBI! Everyone on the floor! Down now!"

Four men followed their supervisor into the apartment, leaving the agent who held the ram to block the doorway.

It took less than a second for King to focus on two targets as they dropped to the floor. A short fat man, on his back, froze after spreading his legs and arms. A young man lay face down with his right arm under his body.

"Show me your hands," the agent next to King yelled as three of his partners ran to check the bathroom and bedroom.

The young man did not respond.

"Your hands! Now!" King shouted.

The young man jerked a small semiautomatic pistol from under his body. King fired a three round burst.

###

Across the Atlantic, a Renault Fourgon windowless delivery truck, with the name of a fictitious bakery painted on the side, pulled to the curb. It parked at the corner of a side street in the Saint-Denis section of north Paris. It was seven in the morning and the driver, in a white uniform, watched the rear view mirror outside his window and held a cell phone in his lap. Behind him, a dark screen obscured the back of the truck.

He was the only man in the truck not wearing the dark blue uniform of the French National Police Intervention Group, and not armed with the futuristic looking, twenty inch long, FN P90 Personal Defense Weapon.

His eyes widened when he saw the car approaching. He lifted the phone, ensuring it remained below the window and cocked his head so the men in the back could hear him. "I see the white car, they're coming. Ten more seconds. I'll tell you when they're beside us."

When the car was ten feet behind the truck, he lowered his head and shouted at the phone. "Block now."

A Mercedes sedan pulled from the side street and blocked the roadway in front of the van. The white car stopped.

"Three bearded men... out now!" the van driver shouted.

The back of the delivery truck opened. Four officers jumped out, surrounded the car and leveled their weapons at the occupants.

National Crime Squad Inspector Ugo Claasen watched his driver turn the unmarked Volvo XC70 onto a dirt road ten miles west of Rotterdam. He glanced over his shoulder. Two constables in a marked white VW Polo patrol car followed, a car-length back. He had waited until the fog lifted but the sun had not yet penetrated the overhanging haze. Ugo had no reservations with his decision to use a small force to take custody of a single old man the surveillance team said was the only one at the farmhouse. Four men would be enough if they were cautious.

Ugo turned to his driver. "Jos?"

He replied without taking his eyes off the road. "Yes?"

"When we get to the house, stop ten or fifteen meters from the front door."

Jos nodded as he stared at the wet dirt and gravel road.

They passed through an open gate at a hedgerow and saw the timeworn, unkempt house. Jos stopped the car well away from the front of the residence and the marked police car pulled alongside the Volvo.

Ugo spotted a bearded old man take a look out a smudged window. He opened the car door, got out and stood behind it. Jos and the two constables followed his lead. One officer ran to the side of the house to observe the back yard.

The front door swung open and the bearded old man, wearing a heavy jacket and baggy pants, stepped into the doorway.

Ugo moved to the leading edge of the car door and glanced at Jos and the officer beside the marked patrol car. "Do not expose yourselves," he said in a low voice.

"Are you Amal?" Ugo called.

"Yes."

"I am Inspector Ugo Claasen of the National Police. You must come with us."

The man stared at him and did not respond.

Ugo paused and glared at the man. "Did you hear what I said?"

"Yes." He raised both his arms above his head and touched his hands together.

Ugo had no time to react when he saw the spark as the man's hands came together. A bright flash and thundering explosion propelled flesh and bone toward the cars.

Carabinieri Lieutenant Vicario, and three of his men, in uniforms with a red stripe down the leg, waited in the secure area past the magnetometers at Rome's Leonardo da Vinci airport.

Plain-clothes officers had followed two Middle Eastern men into the terminal and notified Vicario when they started through security. Taking them into custody outside the airport would have been dangerous. Anti-terrorism investigators from the Special Operations Group told him both men were Al Qaeda operatives. They waited to question them in a nearby room.

Vicario smiled. If he had his way, he'd volunteer for more comfortable assignments like this one. Waiting to confront them behind the security checkpoint, assured the safety of his men.

The Carabinieri stood in a tight group, as if talking, while they watched the two men grab their carry-on luggage and laptop computers. When the men strolled from the secure area, Vicario and his officers approached and took up positions around their targets. "Excuse me. Are you travelling together?" Vicario asked.

"Yes," the one in a gray suit answered.

"What is your name?"

"Fardeen. This is my associate Dahi."

Vicario nodded. "Thank you. I'm Lieutenant Vicario. Both of you are to come with me."

"Is there a problem?" Dahi asked.

"No. Follow me please." He looked at his men. "Take their bags."

Fardeen held up his hand. "Wait!"

Vicario stepped next to him. "At the moment there's no problem, please do as I ask." He began walking. One of his men pointed in the direction Fardeen and Dahi were to take.

"Why are you doing this? I want to talk to your commander," Fardeen said.

Vicario stopped and looked at both men. "I suggest you do not make this difficult for me and my men." He turned and took one-step before Dahi opened his mouth.

"Did you hear him? Where are you taking us?"

Vicario's muscles tightened. He took a deep breath to calm himself. *Is he ignorant or stupid?* "Gentlemen, you can walk with me or I can arrange for stretchers to carry you."

"What's your commander's name?" Fardeen asked.

Vicario smiled. "Follow me. I plan to introduce you to him." The Carabinieri forced them forward.

XXII

THE CHILDREN

A week after the New York and international arrests, Joe and Saleh approached a door in the U. S. District Court building not far from the United States Capitol. Above the frame hung a brass plate with the engraved words 'Grand Jury Waiting Room'. Inside were two coffee tables, two couches and four padded chairs. Styrofoam cups, sugar and creamer sat on a table next to a Keurig coffee maker and a K-Cup carousel.

Saleh crinkled his nose and pointed at the coffee machine. "Black water."

"Americans drink little espresso and Turkish coffee is out of the question."

They unbuttoned their suit jackets and dropped into chairs.

It had been two months since Joe met Saleh in Italy, and most of that time they spent together in the United States. He missed Rome and looked forward to returning in a week. The few people he had to deal with in WITSEC had been friendly and helpful, but he longed for the slow-paced life in Italy and the sight of Nina's face.

"I've seen nothing on the news," Saleh said.

"They're trying to keep it quiet."

Saleh lifted his eyebrows and shook his head. "They won't be able to hide it for long. Akram will know the information is coming from me."

"I'm sure he does."

"You know where they arrested people?"

Joe shrugged. "Agent Zeller said they contacted Italy, England, the Netherlands, Canada, Germany, France and a few more countries."

"What about Saudi Arabia and Iran?"

"The Iranians won't do anything to help. The Saudis said they'd handle their own problems without our help."

Saleh stared at the wall across the room. "I'm sure my old friends already called each other."

"That's good. They can't wait to tell people to protect themselves. Messengers are too slow, and the more phone calls they make, the more information we get. We'll see what happens." Joe pointed to a door with 'Grand Jury Room' printed on it at eye level. "You ready for this?"

Saleh nodded.

"Leonard will ask the questions. Just be honest. The jurors have already heard your name so they shouldn't be surprised when they see you."

"I will."

The Grand Jury room door opened and Angelo, in a dark suit, stepped out and beckoned Saleh. "They want you."

Saleh buttoned his jacket and left Joe and Angelo in the waiting room.

"It's almost over," Joe said after Saleh left the room.

Angelo nodded and sighed. "Good. America is nice but everyone is in a hurry. I'm ready to go home, I miss my family."

"I miss your family too."

Angelo smiled. "We both know why."

The moment Saleh entered the Grand Jury room, every person turned to look at him. Twelve evenly spaced tables stood before him. Most of them occupied by two people with women outnumbering the men.

Assistant U. S. Attorney Leonard Harrison, standing at the front of the room, leaned on a conference table covered with cardboard boxes and file folders. A court reporter sat to his side.

"Come in Mr. al-Filistini." Leonard pointed at the witness box and a high-backed leather chair. "Please stand next to that chair."

From the moment they heard his name, he noticed the jurors watched his every move.

Leonard pointed to a Koran on the corner of the witness box. "Please place your right hand on the Koran."

Saleh complied.

"Please repeat my words. By the right of this, I solemnly swear the testimony I will give is the truth."

Saleh repeated the words.

Earlier that morning, Leonard explained what would happen in the room and had discussed the questions he would ask. Their talk did little to settle the emptiness invading Saleh's stomach.

"Take a seat. I'm Leonard Harrison from the U. S. Attorney's Office."

"Yes, we've met."

Leonard stepped to the large table and leaned against it. "Are you familiar with the American Grand Jury process?"

Saleh shook his head. "Only what you told me."

"Do you recall me explaining the American justice system and the purpose of the grand jury?"

"Yes."

"I told you our sole purpose here was to determine the crimes committed and to discover who should be charged with those crimes, correct?"

"Yes, I understand."

"And I explained that the grand jurors do not convict people... they formalize the charges to be brought against those they think have committed an offense."

"Yes."

"Good. Let's begin." Leonard walked behind the table and opened a file folder. "Please state your name."

Saleh directed his answer to the jurors. "Al-Filistini, Saleh."

"Is that your real name?"

"Yes."

"Are you known by any other names?"

"Yes, Mohammad Halabi."

"Is that all?"

"No. I have passports in two more names. One German and one British."

"And those names are?"

"Omar Jager, and Omar Harrington."

"The first name Omar is on both passports?"

"It's easier to remember."

"During the last seven years were you employed?"

"I have had a job."

"Who did you work for and what position did you hold?"

Saleh hesitated and scanned the jurors. "I worked for Al Qaeda. I planned and organized bombings and murders for them in Europe." Saying those words in front of a group of people felt like admitting he was a barbarian. His heart pounded as he watched the jurors stir, exchange glances and stare at him as if they were eyeball to eyeball with a monster.

"Did you plan and organize terrorist attacks and murders in the United States?"

"I assisted with the plans but didn't organize them."

"Do you recall the terrorist bombing of a bus carrying school children, forty miles outside Vicenza, Italy?"

Saleh looked at the floor. He realized talking about the bombing would not be easy, but didn't expect the question to hit him with the force of a fist smashing into his chest. After taking a deep breath, he raised his head and looked at the jurors. "Yes."

"Do you know if that act of terrorism was an accident?"

"I do." With each response, his heart beat faster.

Leonard hesitated, passing his eyes across the men and women in the room. His speech slowed. "How do you know this?"

"Because I planned it, organized it and watched it happen."

A female juror gasped and covered her mouth.

"Who was the target? Who was supposed to be killed in that attack?"

"American soldiers."

"The children killed, do you know where they were from?"

Saleh exhaled, took a deep breath, and paused. "The Islamic Center School in Milan."

"Milan, Italy?"

"Yes."

"If you planned to kill American soldiers, how did it happen that Muslim children and three adults died?"

"Two buses looked the same. The American bus had a flat tire and stopped. The bus full of children passed the car bomb."

"Your car bomb?"

"No. A man named Pasha put the bomb in the car."

"And who asked him to do that?"

A sinking feeling came over him and he lowered his head. "I did."

"What were the ages of the children on the bus?"

"Eight... ten years old."

A female juror dropped her pencil and covered her mouth with both hands. Leonard waited for her to recover.

"Have you killed or known of other Muslims that were killed by Al Qaeda?"

"Yes. In the Middle East and in Europe."

"Mr. al-Filistini. Were you charged with a crime in Italy, or the United States, for killing forty Muslim children, or attempting to kill thirty-five American soldiers?"

"No."

"Were you told why charges were not brought against you?"

"I agreed to testify and tell Italian and American authorities about the structure and activities of Al Qaeda." Saleh looked at the jurors. Every eye in the room remained locked on him.

"Do you believe you won't be charged with a crime because you agreed to testify?"

Saleh sat erect in the chair. "No. I will be, at a later date."

"If you will be charged with the children's murder, there must be another reason you agreed to testify."

"There is."

"Please explain to the jurors what that reason is."

Saleh slowed his breathing and spoke to the men and women in front of him. "I no longer want to see children killed for a cause that is unattainable."

Leonard stepped closer to the witness box. "What made you reach this decision?"

"Watching Muslim children in Italy die. There can only be one explanation for their bus traveling along that road."

"What is that explanation?"

"A message from the Prophet was sent to me and to all Muslims."

"A message that their cause is unattainable?"

"No, that's not it."

"But you said it was unattainable."

"In a way it is. Non-Muslims around the world will never accept a religion violently forced upon them."

"So you think more people around the world will join in the fight against terrorism?"

Saleh looked at the ceiling and shook his head. *He doesn't understand, no one understands.* "No. They will join in a fight against Islam and the world will suffer."

"How did the death of the forty Muslim children convince you of this?"

"Muslim, Christian, Jewish or even Buddhist... it doesn't matter."

Leonard looked around the room, raised his shoulders and took a deep breath. "What doesn't matter?"

"Their religion doesn't." *Don't you understand?*

"Excuse me, but the jurors may be confused. If al Qaeda's goal is unattainable and their religion doesn't matter, then what does?"

Saleh made eye contact with each juror and lowered his voice. "The children are the ones who matter. They are the world's future."

THE END

www.ingramcontent.com/pod-product-compliance
Lightning Source LLC
Chambersburg PA
CBHW071250130626
46556CB00003B/1245